W9-ASJ-637

Knock at the Door,

EMMY

FLORENCE CRANNELL MEANS

Illustrated by Paul Lantz

HOUGHTON MIFFLIN COMPANY BOSTON

CARNEGIE LIBRARY
LIVINGSTONE COLLEGE
SALISBURY, N. C. 28144

SIXTH PRINTING R

COPYRIGHT © 1956, BY FLORENCE CRANNELL MEANS
ALL RIGHTS RESERVED INCLUDING THE RIGHT TO REPRODUCE
THIS BOOK OR PARTS THEREOF IN ANY FORM
LIBRARY OF CONGRESS CATALOGUE CARD NUMBER 56-5547

PRINTED IN THE U.S.A.

J
813.52
M483

CONTENTS

85211

contents *continued*

Knock at the Door, EMMY

FLORENCE CRANNELL MEANS

Illustrated by Paul Lantz

This book is dedicated to the Miss Marthanns of America, and to the numberless schoolteachers who have opened doors for young hearts and minds even when the young hands have not known how to knock.

Knock at the Door,
E M M Y

1

The Basket Girl

EMMY LANE stepped briskly along the sidewalk, her one unsold basket over her arm. Inside the fence, a tawny dog hurled his heavy body against the pickets, growling and snapping. Emmy hardly noticed him.

Would Pa stop at the Glen? Oh, would he, after all these years? Would Phil Carter still be living there? And would he be as Emmy remembered him? All day those questions had shaken her, had teetered her from joy to despair. By comparison, vicious dogs had no power to move her, and selling baskets was an easy matter, especially when she was on the sky-high end of the teeter.

Only a few years ago she would have been creeping along on frayed canvas shoes, heart pounding with terror under her rough, faded dress, hoping that the next house would have no enemy dog, since, whatever the obstacles, the baskets must be sold.

But now she was almost fifteen. Her crepe-soled blue oxfords were canvas, but they were the kind many girls wore — girls who lived in houses — and so were her jeans and plaid shirt. Further, that shock of dusty-black curls was combed and glistening. She was presentable, and she was a schoolgirl, strange and difficult though her schooling had been. These facts gave her confidence. Much more important, for the first time in six years the Lanes were approaching Glen Lake and Phil Carter.

Maybe Phil Carter, she reminded herself, decisively clicking open the gate. Maybe.

The dog plunged head-on into the unexpectedly opened gate and skidded backward in astonishment. Emmy murmured, "Nice doggy!" and briskly traversed walk and porch steps.

She was thinking that even settled-down folks like Phil's did not always stay in one town all their lives. It had been three years since the last of his letters had caught up with her on her family's continual wanderings. Moreover, Pa might take it into his head not to stop after all, getting his back up the way he did six years ago, mad at Glen Lake and at everybody in it. The thought of not stopping made Emmy swallow convulsively.

As she pressed the bell, the boxer was sniffing at Emmy's ankle socks. Shuffling to the door, an old woman stared at the dog and lifted incredulous, hazy eyes to Emmy's face.

"My land, I never did. Most folks are scared silly at his racket. And he's got real sharp teeth, too."

"Yes, ma'am. I'm used to dogs. You take notice I don't risk my hands in his reach, though. I sure learned that early." The woman sucked in her breath as Emmy turned her right hand, its fingers and palm calloused by basket-weaving, to show the livid scars that puckered it. "Would you care to buy a basket, ma'am? It's my very last one. Kentucky-mountain style; we make them ourselves. Three dollars. This is oak, so there's hardly any wear-out to it. We make willow ones a little cheaper, but these are for the folks that want the best." Admiringly Emmy held up the melon-shaped basket, Pa's pet style.

It was only a few minutes before basket and dollar bills changed hands. With a smiling word of thanks Emmy returned to the gate and latched it after her. "Nice doggy!" she repeated to the boxer, who had followed, still sniffing.

People had always been inclined to buy from Emmy. Pa had put her to peddling when she was six or seven. Then, she thought, people bought because she was little and scared, and because her bright blue eyes were wide and appealing under the tousle of black curls. Dirty! Unkempt! Good gracious, that was the only way Phil Carter had ever seen her, and Phil as clean and combed as it was decent for a boy his age to be. Even his ears looked polished.

The place where the truck would be waiting, with Pa and Ma and maybe Chad, was several blocks away. Emmy did not notice the distance, her thoughts were traveling so much farther.

The Lanes had always shuttled back and forth across the

western half of the country, in a succession of old pickup trucks. When Pa took a notion, they stopped and worked in the crops, especially in the sugar beets in Colorado or the citrus fruits in California. It was in these farm-labor camps, almost as long ago as she could remember, that Emmy had acquired her only girl friend, Refugio Lucero. Even Pa thought the Luceros were decent, as folks went; and Emmy loved Refugio. Though Emmy had always preferred blondes, she thought Refugio the prettest girl in the world, as well as the nicest, with her eyes dark and shining like ripe chokecherries, her hair blue-black, and her features delicately cut.

Pa's regular business, though, was making and selling baskets. For this they settled down only long enough to gather willow and oak and weave the baskets, pausing to peddle them as they passed through towns and villages. Campfires by the roadside, with Ma cooking a little food or opening cans — pallets in the truck except when they were stopping long enough so it was worth while to put up the tent — clothes washed during these longer stops, hung on the tent ropes and put on again rough-dried —

Pa often said exultantly, his deep-set black eyes gleaming, that it was the only free life, and the only one where you could keep yourself to yourself. Pa didn't have much use for folks. When he made camp it was as far as practicable from either hobo jungles or respectable villages, except when they were working in the crops.

Emmy did not share Pa's love of the wandering life. It

was a dusty life, she thought. A chilly, dirty, hot, and sweaty life. Emmy had begun to hate it when Pa first set her to peddling.

"Folks is soft," Pa had answered Ma's feeble objections. "They cain't say no to a peart young one like our Emmy. And it don't hurt her none. Gives her backbone."

So Emmy had scurried along with her oak and willow baskets, her heart shaking her every time she approached any front door, curling up within her when a dog rushed out with bared teeth. First she feared the dogs, and next the little boys, and finally and most of all the little girls. The girls had such a way of looking sidewise at her, taking her in from her wild curls to her dusty canvas shoes and bare legs, and sometimes snickering behind their palms. They were clean little girls, with a polish to them, and with white socks and leather slippers.

All Emmy's hates and fears had come to a climax six years ago, when she was going on nine, and at Glen Lake, now only twenty miles away.

Pa and Ma had pitched tent in a certain hillside clearing and gone off to gather willow, leaving Emmy and five-year-old Chad under strict orders to stay together. This clearing was the only home Emmy knew about, just as Ma's folks were the only family. She had a hazy notion that Pa's folks had been Somebodies back in Kentucky, but Pa wouldn't talk of them. Ma had been raised in this foothill village, in this very clearing. Soon after Ma married and went away her folks died and the house burned down. The stone chimney stood like a tombstone in an oblong a little lower than the surrounding earth.

Emmy was building her doll-baby a playhouse, the way Ma had showed her. Funny how neat Ma could make a playhouse, when she hated real houses so bad. The doll-baby was one Emmy had found on a town dump, source of many treasures. It had nothing wrong with it except the loss of its wig and of the elasticity of its rubber-strung joints. Pa had got interested, as he sometimes did when clever fingers were needed. He had cut strips from an old leather jacket, also picked up on the dump, soaked the strips well, and strung them through the doll's joints. At first the puppet lay every which way, and Emmy was discouraged. Her disappointment turned to joy, for the drying leather shrank, and the doll jerked to life. To hide the doll's baldness, Emmy clumsily stitched a bonnet from a rag she found, and a dress to make the child decent. She loved her baby with all her turbulent heart.

That long-ago day she had looked up from doll and playhouse and had missed her brother. Pa would sure whale tar out of Chad if he knowed he'd run off like that, she thought. She had scrambled up to look for him when he came struggling and panting into the clearing.

"They got a birthday party," he gasped, jerking his head backward. "Girl, name of Abbie Allen. Games. Ice cream. Ast us to come."

Emmy would never forget her astonishment. "Charles Lane Junior, what a whopper!"

Vigorously Chad shook his head. "Little boy. Littler'n me. Says, 'You come, too.' I says, 'And my sis?' And he says, 'Sure.' He ast us."

Emmy was already on her feet, after disposing the doll carefully in its playhouse. Maybe miracles still happened, like Pa said they use' to in the Good Book. Chad hardly ever storied. "Honest and true, Chad, black and blue, lay me down and cut me in two?" she quavered, her blue eyes boring into his deep-set brown ones.

When Chad nodded vehemently, Emmy dashed into the tent, threw open the old trunk, rummaged through it for her best dress. Ma had bought it at a rummage sale, and it was beautiful, though made for a girl two years larger. Emmy also pulled out a clean shirt and pair of pants for Chad, and flung them backward at him. Both children put on the fresh clothes over what they were wearing. Then, her brother's face and hands catching her attention, Emmy filled a tin basin from the bucket, laid hold on Chad, and scoured him till areas emerged startlingly clean. As energetically she went over the high spots on her own face and washed her hands up to the wrists. Chad's hair was cropped short and no bother, and Emmy had never thought about her own. Nor about ears. So they were ready.

"But — you got to take a present," she remembered suddenly. Ma had once told her about parties.

"Mebbe we best not go," Chad muttered, in a tone of mild panic.

"Baskets make nice presents," Emmy said, unheeding, and pounced on a fancy little willow one.

Six years had dimmed some memories, while they left others larger and clearer than life, partly because Emmy had long, jogging hours on the truck to think about them. This side of the church Abbie Allen's house was, all shiny mustard yellow and fenced with white that had not a picket missing. A pony was tied to the fence, and in the

yard were slick starched children. They stopped their singsong play on the green lawn and stood staring as Emmy unlatched the gate and went up the walk, Chad behind, holding to her dress.

Up glossy gray-painted steps to a screen door where Emmy pressed the bell — the click of heels inside, and a woman staring down through the screen from pale blue eyes. "Oh, baskets. How much, little girl?"

Emmy shook her head, moistened her lips. "A present. For Abbie. We come to the party."

The china-blue eyes rounded until a white rim circled them. Emmy could not recall the woman's words, but her headshake was a decided negative. While Emmy stood frozen, with Chad tugging at her and breathing noisily, the woman clicked across the room again, clicked back with a covered bowl and a paper bag, which she thrust at Emmy through a crack barely wide enough. They weren't to bother to fetch back the bowl. It was a chipped one. Her teeth showed like white china, a great many of them.

Emmy could never think how she reached the gate, with Chad almost falling off the porch when she turned in her blind hurry, and treading so close that he stepped on her heel and pulled one of her sneakers half off. Except for subdued snickers, the children were silent watchers. One fair boy, taller than Emmy, stood a little in advance of the rest, intently gazing, while a little fellow peered out from behind him as if perhaps he had been the one who asked Chad to come.

Outside the gate Emmy was forced to stop. She had to set down bowl, bag, and basket, both to readjust the canvas shoe and to latch the gate. She had to latch that gate; had to.

The pony proved an ally, nuzzling her neck while she groped at the latch. Deliberately then Emmy took a cooky from the bag and fed it to the little beast. Its soft wheedling lips gave Emmy comfort, and also time to control her shaking hands and twisting mouth. She did not look up till a boy's voice spoke from the front of the crowd of children. It was the voice of the fair boy who had stared, and it sounded mad, but not at Emmy.

"Looky," he said, "Star likes you. And let me tell you, Star's choosy. She doesn't cotton to any of the Glen kids. What's your name, kid, huh? What's your name?"

"Emmy Lou Lane," she muttered. Then she settled the basket on her arm, crowded the bowl into it, picked up the paper bag, and turned her face homeward. Behind her Chad sniffled and snorted and dragged her long dress awkwardly round her legs.

Emmy remembered that the truck was already in the clearing when the two reached it, and she hung back, not knowing how to explain events. Chad had no hesitation. He ran howling to his mother and butted her in the middle with his little cropped head.

Emmy spoke dully. "He said they ast us and they never. It was a party, and Chad said they ast us, but they never."

"He did so! That little old boy — " Chad whimpered, like one betrayed.

Pa strode forward, face contorted, and snatched basket, bowl, and bag. The bag and bowl he flung to the ground outside the clearing, and the basket he ground into the earth with a furious heel. "Don't you never ask me to come to this place again!" he gritted at Ma, using other words that he seldom let fly. Pa could get red hot in a flash. Emmy took his ungovernable temper for granted, because she had the same kind. Pa often said, with an inverted pride, that she could throw a tantrum at the drop of a hat.

Pa and Ma were away again next morning when the sorrel pony picked its way into the clearing. Chad twisted around where he was hunkered down on the ground over some play of his own, but Emmy, after a single glance, turned her back and went on washing the few breakfast dishes, as if the world held nothing but the disreputable pan and the odds and ends of tinware. This was another picture that had remained clear and whole to Emmy, though perhaps she had added to it or taken from it in reliving it so long.

"Hi!" shouted the boy. "Emmy Lou Lane! You know what? My mom knew your mom when she was a kid. Honest."

Emmy only hunched her shoulders lower over the battered dishpan. Tears of shame blinded her, for this boy had witnessed their rejection.

When she did not respond, Phil tried his luck with Chad. "Cat got her tongue, huh? What's your name? Mine's Phil, Phil Carter."

Since Chad copied his sister's silence, she muttered, "Chad. Charles Lane Junior." Those tears thickened her voice.

"Look!" Phil protested in alarm. "You don't feel bad about — about yesterday? That old Mis' Allen," he added gruffly, "she can't stand for anybody to be prettier and nicer than her old Abbie."

Emmy lifted a ragged elbow to rub her wet nose and eyes.

Phil tried again. "Look, kid. I got something for you."

Thus forced to look around, Emmy saw that Phil was holding out a book, a chunky book done up in a cover of red-checked cloth. He laughed at her surprise.

"Mom borrowed it from your mom when she was just a kid," he explained, still laughing at Emmy's blank expression. "All these years she's been mad because she forgot to give it back. But that isn't the funniest." He chirped to the mare to advance, and then leaned over to open the book and show Emmy the flyleaf. Emmy stared uncomprehendingly at black letters which said nothing at all to her. "*Emmy Lou!*" he said triumphantly. "Mom says millions of folks named their kids after this book. It's got keen stories, even if they are about a girl. You read it and tell me if you don't think it's swell."

Emmy wiped her hands on the dishrag and then on her

dress and took the book. Bending over it as if reading that title page, she was choked with gratitude that Chad was no talker. He would not tell this boy that his sister could not read a word, did not know her alphabet, even if she was near nine years old.

The boy said, "I'll come back real soon and see how you liked it."

Emmy shook her head, looking up at him through her lashes. "We're pulling out first off in the morning. Us Lanes, we like to keep on the go."

"Shucks. Well, look. Write me a letter soon as you've read it. I'll answer if you tell me where."

"Where do you live?" Emmy asked shyly.

Phil gestured down toward the log church. "Right past the parsonage. The Glen doesn't have city street numbers. Just put Phil Carter, Glen Lake, Colorado."

He was staring at her as if he liked her. As if she looked nice, even though she wasn't smooth and clean like the girls at the party. Even if she was plumb ignorant and would always be.

Because how could a kid ever get book-learning when her folks went banging all over the country in a pickup? You couldn't go to school when you moved every day or two. Ma had said so with dreary flatness once when Emmy mentioned school, and Pa had made the same answer with impatient finality. But this was the first time in Emmy's nine years that the realization had settled on her spirit like a rockslide that would bury her alive.

"Mooning!" the going-on-fifteen Emmy accused herself under her breath, and laughed softly. The mooning had taken her over the blocks to the pickup, parked in the shade of a big cottonwood. Waiting in it were Pa and Ma and Chad, dusty, tired people, grimed and crumpled from travel.

Pa stretched his bony body, yawning violently. "Got rid of the whole bunch!" he commented. "Say, you kids sell 'em fastern'n we can make 'em. Cleaned us out."

Emmy's heart jumped and she spoke in a tone carefully casual. "Good thing we're so close to Glen Lake. Lots of willows, even if not oak."

Pa frowned, but before he could say anything, Emmy said quickly, "Pa, you look like you was asleep sitting up. Whyn't you stretch out and get a cat nap while I drive?"

For an anguished moment Emmy expected him to say, "No Glen Lake, understand, missy?" But sleep was heavy upon him and for the time overcame his opposition. His mouth twisted in another monstrous yawn and he swung his feet over into the truck bed and slipped down among the dingy household gear that cluttered it.

Emmy could drive as good as anybody, Pa said, and with him in the truck and Ma in the seat — even if Ma never had learned to drive — it was all legal enough if the cops didn't get too nosy. Pa never could stand to have anybody, even the law, try to boss him in his own car.

So Emmy drove the crotchety old truck along the highway between lofty sculptured rocks and mesas toward Glen Lake, her hope mounting as the road did. Here the evergreen fragrances were distilled by the hot sun, so that they almost overcame the acrid fumes from the laboring truck; and right ahead was the point where the Glen Lake road branched off from the main highway.

Emmy cast a quick glance over her shoulder at Pa. His felt hat, faded and streaked with long use, was pulled down over his eyes, and his stubbly lips and cheeks puffed out, drew in, with the peaceful regularity of sleep.

Holding her breath, Emmy turned the truck to the left, onto the Glen road. Ma stirred uneasily and Chad made a gruff little sound in his throat, but nobody spoke. Only when the truck swooped sharply to the underpass beyond Obelisk, three miles short of Glen Lake, did Pa sit up, blinking.

"Now who told you — ? Now who the dickens ever give you the idea — ?" Pa rumbled.

"Oh, didn't you mean for us to stop and get willows?" Emmy asked, quickening her speed and keeping her eyes on the road.

Pa grunted. "I'll take her now," he said sourly, and climbed over as soon as Emmy had drawn up on a firm shoulder.

Emmy sat in the back with her arms clasping her blue-jean knees while Pa expertly guided the old truck over the three dipping, soaring miles to the crossroad which was

Glen Lake's business center. Emmy moistened her dry lips and clenched her fists till the stubby nails bit her calloused palms. Her held breath hurt her lungs.

For five of the past six years she had been building up the picture of herself coming back to Glen Lake, coming back and showing Phil Carter how much she had changed from the dirty ragamuffin of nine. If Phil was still there.

And now it was a fifty-fifty chance that Pa would drive right on through the village and out the farmers' road to the highway. There were plenty of willows along the farmers' road without having to stop in the clearing.

2

The Meeting

MA'S THOUGHTS must have been running parallel to Emmy's. She spoke in the rusty, breathless voice of one who does not talk much. "Pa — the folks' graves — been so long — "

Pa let out an explosive breath. "Well, have it yore own way," he grumbled, and swerved the truck past the stores and post office to the road that climbed the lower slopes of the hill behind the village. Emmy's eyes went weakly shut and her breath came out in a great gust that left her collapsed.

She got her eyes open in time to see the mustard-yellow Allen house, where the party had been, and the Little Log Church and parsonage. Next door to the parsonage, Phil had said. The house next door was white. Emmy was glad it was white. It set off the bright green grass and the colors of the irises and climbing roses. But none of this told her whether Phil still lived there.

"Got to admit," Pa grudged, "the old sky ain't never

quite so blue as it is right here. Bluest behind red old Chautauqua."

"I'd forgotten it was all so pretty," said Emmy.

She'd even forgotten how golden red that rugged rock face of the mountain could shine in the sun, and how the yucca blossomed like fat white candles up and down the hills while larkspur bloomed blue in sheltered places. The tips of the evergreens held grosbeaks, pouring out their varied song. Always nabbed on to the highest spots they could find, Pa said, so nobody would miss them.

The Lanes were unconsciously sitting forward and holding their breath, for it was always nip and tuck, as Pa muttered, whether the truck would make the last steep grade. Pa never could get any but the cheapest old trucks, but he was so smart about tinkering them that they gave him a lot of mileage. He always picked out Fords and Chevvies and such, so that he could be sure to find spare parts at any junkyard or even sometimes on the dump.

The clearing was beautiful, too. As they pulled into it, a small, sweet song welcomed them, and Emmy's quick eyes found the singer in a thicket of scrub oak and choke-cherry, a little olive-green bird with a red cap and a white bib. Ma brought out the old bird cage, which was such a point of contention with Pa. She hung it in a sunny scrub oak and unpinned the rag that swathed it.

"Think that there wild bird will learn yours to sing?" Pa scoffed.

Pet, Ma's old canary, sat humped on his perch. When he felt the sun he shook himself until he almost lost his balance, but remained mute.

Emmy and Chad had grabbed buckets, as they always did when they stopped anywhere to cook or sleep, and had gone to find water. Here the brook was near at hand and they were soon back. Firewood they could gather later, for there was plenty of dry brush.

Pa said, "Reckon I better get on down to the store and lay in some grub."

Heart jumping again, Emmy swung herself into the seat with Chad, and Pa tooled the truck around and downhill. Emmy kept looking from side to side, but saw no one she knew.

The old store, smelling of coffee and spices and bread, had been changed around to look more like a city market. Magazines were spread invitingly in the window, visible from inside and out, and a poster which Emmy read with quickening interest. It was signed "Marthann Spencer," and announced "Vacation School at the Little Log Church. Children from Six to Sixteen Welcome."

The store lady saw Emmy peering at the sign and said, "Miss Marthann is our minister."

Pa snorted. "Petticoat preacher, huh? New style, I reckon. Got any old-style soupbones, without all the meat took off?"

The store lady said yes, she thought they had a good

shank, and added that the Glen wouldn't trade Miss Marthann for any two men ministers. Besides, she said, Miss Marthann was a Quaker.

"Reckon that makes some difference," Pa admitted.

"If you're staying awhile, your girl might like to go to the vacation school. Or is she past sixteen?" the store lady added as an afterthought, studying Emmy with smiling gray eyes from behind the meat counter.

Emmy flushed as at a compliment and was tongue-tied.

"Going on fifteen, ma'am, though if you was to hear her read you'd say she was twenty. But—vacation school: I reckon not. First place, she don't need such as that. Second place, us Lanes never sets long in one spot. We like to travel."

"Lane?" asked the store lady. "The basket man! I didn't place you. Haven't seen you for years, have I? Do you still carry those oak-splint baskets, sort of melon shape? Customers are always trying to coax me to sell mine." She nodded sidewise toward one of Pa's specials, filled with white lilacs. "I'd buy half a dozen, if the price was right."

"Sorry. Plumb out of that kind."

The store lady made a rueful mouth.

"I got enough oak, I reckon," Pa said slowly, evidently pleased by her liking his favorite baskets. "Guess I could make you some. The wife kind of likes to stop here awhile."

Next morning Emmy and Chad presented themselves at

the Little Log Church at the hour the poster mentioned. Both wore clean blue jeans that hadn't begun to need patching, and plaid shirts that hadn't begun to fade. Chad's hair was still cropped but Emmy's had become a decorative item. Combing it with a wet comb made every lock curl. She could tie a ribbon wherever it happened to be the fashion, and even Chad said it looked all right, sliding an unwilling glance of admiration at it.

The school was made up of children from summer colony, village, and surrounding ranches, and most of them wore jeans, so that Emmy and Chad looked no different from the rest. Opening exercises were held in the auditorium before classes separated. Emmy sang happily with the others, quickly catching on to the tunes. Though it didn't have the pictured glass windows Emmy had so often read about, this was a church, and she had never been inside a church before.

For classes the big boys and girls went into the schoolhouse across the road, and Emmy liked that, too. The smells of chalk dust and scrubbed floors always exhilarated her. Yet her mind was not fully on any of the songs and drills of the morning program. At once she had looked around with swift scrutiny to see who was there. Her heart skipped a beat at sight of a fair-haired little boy, and then she realized disappointedly that he was the size Phil Carter had been six years ago.

Again her pulse skipped a few beats when a blond head

passed the classroom windows, high enough up to be fourteen or fifteen. But when the head was turned, Emmy saw that the eyes were brown.

While the class was working on spatter prints for the covers of the vacation school scrapbooks, Emmy screwed up her courage. She rose and started toward the desk and Miss Selby, a faded middle-aged woman with firmly corrugated gray hair. Emmy meant to ask whether a boy named Phil Carter came to that school. Halfway up the aisle she altered the question. She would say, "Excuse me, but does Abbie Allen come to this school?" And she would add, with indifferent lightness, "Or a boy named Phil Carter? I met him once at her house."

At the last minute her courage came unscrewed. She held out the lacy leaf Miss Selby had given her for her spatter print, and said, "Please, ma'am, could you tell me the name of this plant?"

To her discomfort, Miss Selby stopped everything and spoke to the class. "Boys and girls!" she exclaimed dramatically, her rimless glasses coming loose and having to be pinched back on her thin nose. "Boys and girls, do you know something?"

Out of teen-age titters and snickers a voice piped, "Sure we don't, teacher. That's why we came to school."

Miss Selby primmed her lips and ignored the pleasantry. "This is the very first young person who has asked the name of a single plant among the dozens I gathered for you."

"Do we have to be introduced to them to make it legal?" an uncertain young bass asked innocently.

Miss Selby's lips stretched in a pained smile. "Very funny. But there is such a thing as intellectual curiosity, class. When we cease to be intellectually curious we cease to grow. Here, my dear, is a book, a key to Colorado wild flowers. Find the name for yourself and it will be worth a great deal more than my telling you. I'll give you one clue," she added, pursing her lips and looking arch. "It grows tall and carries its flowers like white lace umbrellas."

"That gimmick's so old it's got a beard on it," whispered the boy behind Emmy, as she sat down with the book. "Bet you two bits she doesn't know the name herself."

Emmy settled herself to track down her leaf, almost forgetting, in the interest of the hunt, what she had really wanted to ask. All books were wonderful, and this was her first experience in asking one for a plant name. The search gave her a sense of power, of having in her hands the key to the universe.

When Miss Selby minced down the aisle, toes pointed primly outward, checking on the spatter prints, Emmy had barely begun hers.

She lifted eager eyes. "This looks to me — " she said shyly, pressing a finger on the page. "Or this — "

Miss Selby clapped her hands and blinked her eyes delightedly. "You're right! It's angelica! Class, isn't that an enchanting name? It's related to the cow parsnip, as the book says, and to the poison hemlock, and a country cousin to Queen Anne's lace."

Chad's class had assembled in Miss Marthann's house, and both Ma and Emmy asked him about it that noon.

"It was okay," Chad said. "Sat round a big table, newspapers on it. Made bears out of plaster. Neat."

"What kind of house?" Emmy pressed him yearningly. "From outside I could see curtains kind of between pink and yellow, with ruffles in little straight folds, like."

"Pleats," said Ma.

"What else d'you see?" Emmy persisted. Houses — they were as magical as schools.

Scowling, Chad scuffed a sneaker in the dust. "Aw — lots of plants. And a pi-ano."

They could pry nothing more out of him.

"Well, did you see anyone you knew?" Emmy tried another line of attack.

"Don't know nobody," Chad said in surprise.

"The boy who rode the sorrel pony?" Emmy prompted. Perceiving the blankness of his stare, she did swift calculation. Chad had been five. People did forget things that happened when they were so young.

That afternoon all the Lanes worked on baskets, but along toward five o'clock Pa put the stuff aside and went fishing, accompanied by Chad. Ma began the supper, for Pa had fetched stew meat from the store today, and it took more time than canned food.

Emmy wandered around the clearing, looking down on the village from the highest point. She could see the church, across from the schoolhouse, and next to it Miss Marthann's house, the parsonage, and beyond it the white house with the old-fashioned porches. From its back chimney a line of smoke rose straight into the pale blue sky of afternoon. Someone was in the house, but the smoke did not disclose, any more than the lawn and garden had, whether it was the Carters or just — folks.

Next Emmy strolled down the dimly marked road. When afoot she had Pa's habit of looking for crystals and arrowheads and the like, and Ma's way of looking for flowers. Emmy picked fluffy cream-colored spikes from the wild spiraea bushes, and added sprays of the gilia, which Ma called coral blossoms. In spite of Ma's dislike for a stationary home, whenever they stopped for a day she did fancy having flowers stuck in a bottle, where she could see and smell them.

Even the flowers did not make Emmy as happy as she had expected to be, nor the sweetness of the air. Glen Lake was too empty.

She had turned back toward the tent when a soft whinny behind her whirled her around, unbelieving. A slender sorrel mare was picking her way over the rough road. A fair-haired boy bestrode her, and a curly black dog jogged close behind.

Emmy stood rooted, the mass of flowers clutched to her breast like a shield. *I can't say a word, not to save me. But,*

oh, am I thankful he didn't come closer to the tent. Messy, the tent is; the whole clearing.

The mare stopped a few feet short of Emmy. The little

black dog sat down abruptly and panted, tongue out. Emmy just stood, and Phil just sat.

His Adam's apple's going up and down. He's as scared as me. The thought steadied Emmy. "I thought I'd pick some flowers for Ma," she managed to say.

"Pretty. Pretty as anything," Phil said with a gulp.

Emmy glanced at him again. He wasn't looking at the flowers, but at her, and his gray-blue eyes were clear and steady and smiling a little, as if she looked even nicer than he had expected.

"Gosh, but you've grown," he said. "I kind of thought of you the size you used to be." He stretched a hand down to indicate a midget's height. "Still and all, I'd have known you anywhere. The curls and eyes."

"Do you think I've grown more than you have?" Emmy asked, stooping to pat the dog and gently twist its ears, as Pa had told her they liked.

For answer, Phil swung himself from the saddle and stretched to his full height. "Mom says I'd be a right tall man if so much of me wasn't turned up at one end," he joked, sticking out a big boot.

Emmy was glad of something to laugh at. She was embarrassed at having stared as she had done. After six years, though, when her memory of him would never come quite clear, how could she help staring? She was not disappointed in what she saw: blue-gray eyes rather wide-set; a cowlick at one temple that kept his fair hair from parting straight; the hair darker than she remembered, a sort of rusty gold, streaked lighter on top by the sun; a mouth older, firmer, straighter.

"How did you know we were here?" Emmy asked out of a long silence.

"Miss Marthann. She said you came to vacation school this morning."

"I thought maybe you'd be there." Emmy tried to sound completely indifferent. "And Abbie Allen. Does she still live in the Glen?"

"Abbie? Oh, sure. Calls herself Gail now. Name's Abigail. Both of us went to vacation school every summer since we were little kids. Decided we'd call it a day."

Emmy felt better when Phil went on to say, "Miss Marthann was telling me this morning, though, she wished I'd help out with the rowdy little kids. So I said okay, I guessed I could stand two weeks of it."

Emmy felt a giggle coming on, and hoped Phil would not guess that it was a giggle of happiness. She smelled the bouquet and pretended to sneeze, and laughed, and Phil laughed with her.

"Gosh," he said, "but five years was a long time."

"Six," Emmy corrected him.

3

Sunshine and Storm

For Emmy that week was sunshine without shadow. She had forgotten how good it was to be at Glen Lake. Or maybe it had never been so lovely as this year. When she got up in the morning it was cool and all kinds of birds were singing, and Emmy hurried to pull the bedding out of the tent and spread it on the bushes to air. Toward noon the sun-warmed pines filled the air with fragrance. As soon as the afternoon sun had dipped behind Sundance Mountain the crisp freshness made Emmy want to walk a mile.

Even Ma chirked up a little in the cool high altitude. She washed a few things and tidied the tent. It was almost impossible to keep neat when you were jogging along day after day in a truck.

Ma not only cooked a real stew, with the meat and potatoes Pa had brought, and the onions, simmering them long and deliciously after she had browned them. She also made dumplings to go on top. Pa sniffed with pleasure and licked his lips at the fragrance of that sleepily simmering kettle.

"This here is like you use' to cook, Ma. Long time ago."

Ma said, "The place put me in mind of my mother's Irish stew and dumplings. 'First give it a taste of the fire,' she used to say, 'before you put in the water.' "

Emmy thought, Ma's lively today, for her. And she really used to be different. Not just my imagining things. It's as if her elastic had lost its strength little by little, the way my old doll's did. Up here it tightens the least bit.

Still more fascinating than the clearing was the vacation school. It was packed with fun and with learning new things. And everything was better because Phil appeared now and then, so you never knew when to expect him, since he was helping Miss Marthann rather than attending classes. It was both exciting and restful, Emmy thought, to catch sight of his tall, funnily lanky figure, which hadn't begun to fill out yet. Emmy would feel the same happiness if it were Refugio Lucero instead of Phil Carter, she told herself positively. She wanted no boy-and-girl nonsense. Not yet.

But when a girl was going on fifteen and had never had but two friends, she naturally prized those two. Yes, she felt exactly the same about Phil as about Refugio. Only different.

Friday noon the vacation school picnicked down at the old campground, under the narrow-leaf aspens and spruces, amid spiraea, harebell and other wild flowers—and plenty of poison ivy. Abbie Allen came to the picnic. She said she did not recall ever having seen Emmy before, and Emmy was thankful for her forgetfulness. Abbie had grown much prettier than the picture in Emmy's memory.

Emmy couldn't keep from looking at her, small and dainty, like one of the miniature dolls that sat in boxes in store windows, delicate arms appealingly spread and fluffy skirts billowing around them. Nobody ought to be quite so la-di-da for a picnic, Emmy thought crossly. To be sure, Abbie wore jeans, but they were as new as fresh paint, and managed to look prim, as well as slim and tiny. Abbie's silky hair was fluffed like an expensive doll's hair, and her coloring was the peachy blondness that was Emmy's ideal.

Emmy tried to hide her lunch of stout bologna sandwiches wrapped in bread papers. Phil took one and said it was a dandy, but he said the same about Abbie's thin little affairs, frilled with lettuce and wrapped in smooth waxed paper. He cut his big slab of homemade cake in two and gave half to Emmy and half to Abbie.

Another of Glen Lake's attractions was the library, which filled a small room between Miss Marthann's study and the church itself, and was open to all comers.

To Emmy it was Aladdin's lamp. On Saturday morning she tiptoed from shelf to shelf, reading the titles and pulling out a book here, a book there, opening them and forgetting everything else as she read. Miss Marthann's door was ajar, and Emmy could see her working at her desk, a funny kind of minister, in bluejeans and a plaid shirt because she had gone up the canyon before breakfast to fish.

Absent-mindedly she looked out into the library. When she saw Emmy, her face lighted and warmed as if Emmy really amounted to something. "You know," she called in her soft, high voice, "all you have to do is put down your name and what books you're checking out, Emmy," and went back to her work again.

Emmy could take books home!

Next day Emmy and Chad went to church. It was their first church service, but they sat part-way back and Emmy got along without trouble by watching what other people did. Flowers were massed at the altar, lilacs and irises and wild spiraea. Outside the window the meadows dropped away to the town, and the town dropped away to the ravine, and on the far side rose the mountain, thick with evergreens. Beyond its shoulder the plains stretched on and on, pine forests inky dark on the horizon, and the sun glittering on windshields and rear windows of automobiles that came and went in swift procession along the looping highway.

A visiting minister was preaching that day, and Emmy lost track of his sermon except when he repeated one statement that seemed as if aimed straight at her. Each time he said it, Emmy sat straighter, with a twitch of astonishment. "Seek, and ye shall find," he said. "Knock, and it shall be opened unto you."

It was the knocking part that sent a chill of joyous amazement down Emmy's spine, for it was knocking that had changed life for her.

The congregation was not entirely strange to the young Lanes. Boys and girls who attended the vacation school were there. On the platform sat Miss Marthann, face serene above her ministerial robe, but smiles waiting in hazel eyes and folded lips. Miss Selby, wearing a marvelous hat, was in a pew near the front, and Abbie Allen, more than ever like a doll, in the young people's choir. Across the narrow aisle from Emmy and Chad were the Carters. Emmy tried not to look at them, but she liked to watch Phil hunt up the hymn and offer his parents the open book.

As soon as the pianist had played a last number, Emmy and Chad scurried out. Phil caught up with them on the lawn, and his voice squeaked high and plunged low, as if he, too, were nervous.

"Emmy, Mom wants to meet you two kids. She knew your mother — remember?"

The three of them waited in the shade of a tree, Emmy feeling conspicuous, especially when Abbie Allen floated out with other members of the choir. Emmy thought miserably that her own skirt and blouse were clumsy in comparison with the blown-glass delicacy of Abbie's dress.

"Hi, Phil!" Abbie called gaily. "Oh, hello, Emmy."

Phil said, "Hi, Gail," and looked beyond her at the door.

Mrs. Carter was there, turning back for another word with Miss Marthann in her black robe, and then coming down the steps smiling. She was taller than Emmy, and strongly built. Since Emmy had always preferred blondes, she couldn't decide whether to call Mrs. Carter handsome, but she was definitely a pleasure to see. Her skin was weathered by Colorado's strong sun and wind, and smile wrinkles rayed out from the warm brown eyes that had sought Emmy out at once. Emmy thought her smile was her only resemblance to Phil. For the most part he had taken after his father, a tall, slender man with sun-streaked fair hair, looking over his wife's head with blue eyes that narrowed against the light.

"Mom," Phil was saying, "this is Emmy Lou Lane. And Chad. And my pop, Emmy."

Mrs. Carter took Emmy's hand in both of hers and smiled down at her. "You children must favor your father. Yet there's a look of my old friend in you, Emmy. Maybe it's those eyes, so blue when you'd expect brown."

Emmy felt suddenly secure from all the curious glances that touched her.

"Has Phil asked you if you'd all come to dinner with us?" Mrs. Carter went on. "You'll have to excuse the last-minute invitation, but we weren't sure a whole houseful of company wasn't coming from Denver this morning. Too many for our chairs and tables."

Emmy caught her breath. "Thank you, ma'am, Mrs. Carter. Pa and Ma — I'm afraid not. But I'll go ask."

In another minute Phil was walking home with her and Chad, and she was wondering uneasily how Pa and Ma would be looking and what they would say.

As usual, Pa was tinkering with the truck, this time

putting a boot into one frail, collapsed tire. He had taken Ma to the burying ground with some posies, he said, greeting the young people, and had got a flat tire as they returned to the clearing.

Emmy's glance flew to her mother. Ma had worn her best clothes to the cemetery and had not yet changed back. Thinking how she would seem to Phil, Emmy thought that she was shabby but neat enough; how bent, though, and how unsmiling! Yet the face was a gentle one, and the eyes might have been like Emmy's when she was young: blue, someone had once said of Emmy's, so light and bright that it resembled a sunny mountain lake.

Politely Phil was asking, "Mom says, won't you all come to dinner with us, Mrs. Lane?" Boyishly he added, "We're having fried chicken and Mom's angel food and ice cream."

Chad was muttering to his mother, his dark little face crimsoned.

Ma said, "Hush!" and then, to Phil, "Chad — maybe he best not. And Pa and me — I — I guess we couldn't hardly — but Emmy — thank you. Your mother was always — "

Emmy lingered a moment, eyes fixed on Ma. Her gaze seemed momentarily to dispel Ma's vagueness. She said, "Your hair ribbon, Emmy," and reached up to straighten its loops. And while she was close to Emmy, closer than usual in every way, "Just watch her, honey. Do like her."

As they started away, Emmy wanted two opposite

things. She wanted to prolong the walk, both because she was scared and because she was happy. And she wanted to hurry and see the Carter house, which she had so often dreamed about.

When Phil ushered her into its enveloping smells of cleanness and lilacs and food, she tried to look every way at once without seeming to, her heart thudding with excitement. The house had not the glitter of wood surfaces she had observed at the Allens' on that memorable day. It had big, comfortable-looking chairs, and bookcases, and magazines on the table, and lilacs in a bowl on the piano. Looking at it, Emmy ached with longing, it was so different from a home in a tent and a truck.

Turning in another direction she was startled to encounter a girl and boy so close at hand that she jerked away from them. Then she giggled at her own mistake. "I never saw it was a looking glass — such a great big looking glass — "

"I got my suspicions about that glass. I think Mom hopes it will keep Pop and me tidier, staring at us the way it does." Phil stroked back his hair, but his eyes gazed out of the mirror, straight into Emmy's. "We look a pair," he blurted, hastening to add, "You know what, Emmy? We're both going to be mighty tall when we get our growth."

He was perhaps two inches taller than she, though his lankiness magnified the difference. Emmy's glance pulled away from his and coasted down her own reflection, much clearer than in store windows. Her skirt didn't hang quite straight, but it wasn't bad. Though not daintily miniature like Abbie Allen, she was slim, and her black curls and red-brown tan made her blue eyes shine as if they had a light behind them. She didn't look the way Abbie did, as if she were soaked in sweet-smelling soapsuds every blessed day; but she was a good, practical, camping-out clean. She sighed. Goodness knows, it took a heap of work to attain even that degree of grooming. Yet lots of other girls, like Refugio for instance, kept themselves just as clean and smart while living in tents or shacks.

Mrs. Carter came to the door and said, "Oh, did you two get ahead of the others?" When they both explained at once, she said, "Oh dear! Maybe another time, then. We'll be ready to sit down, in a minute."

Emmy could hardly see the table at first, because Phil was pulling back her chair and she had no idea what she was supposed to do about it.

Mrs. Carter filled in the awkward moment, speaking with mock severity. "Papa, will you ever learn modern manners from your son? I like to be put in, too."

"Mamma," he grumbled, "you shouldn't try to teach an old dog new tricks. Oh, well!" He strode around from his end of the table and drew out her chair, one of his big-jointed freckled hands patting her shoulder as he did so.

Closely watching, Emmy imitated Mrs. Carter, even to the little hitching lift she gave herself as the chair slid forward. That was safely over, but the next minute Emmy barely missed making a blunder. She had opened her mouth to say politely that it was a very nice day, when suddenly all the other eyes went shut, and Mr. Carter murmured words Emmy couldn't make out.

Immediately thereafter he addressed himself to the platter of crusty brown chicken before him, and the bowls of swirled white mashed potatoes, gilded with melted butter, and of green peas, and of gravy. First he served Mrs. Carter. Emmy made a note of the fact that the mother was supposed to be served first. Wouldn't Pa grunt at that notion! Then Mr. Carter tipped his head back to get a better look through his glasses, and asked, "Now what kind of meat would Miss Emmy prefer?"

Embarrassment made Emmy's voice squeak like a boy's. "Just any — any kind, sir." She was casting quick glances at Mrs. Carter, to see which fork she would take, and how she would handle it, but Mrs. Carter was busy with cups and coffeepot.

"This is Postum, not real coffee," she told Emmy, as if misinterpreting the question in her eyes.

Dinner was not an unbearable ordeal, after all, though the Carters all held their silver in a way strange to Emmy. She ate slowly, copying Mrs. Carter, and the Carters talked and laughed so much that she gradually lost her embarrassment. The main dishes were deliciously seasoned and hot, and the salad deliciously seasoned and cool. Yet the greatest novelty to Emmy was the table setting, with an embroidered mat at each place, flowers in the middle and an abundance of shining silver.

Once she stopped eating to gaze unconsciously at the sideboard behind Phil, who sat opposite her. Silver candlesticks flanked a silver bowl of wild flowers. She had seen pictures of such sideboards in the grocery magazine and in half-burned *Journals* and *Companions* retrieved from the dump, but she hadn't taken much stock in them.

"Lost your appetite, Miss Emmy?" Mr. Carter teased her. "Or did you find a lump in Mamma's mashed potatoes?"

"Oh — oh, no, sir. They're — perfect. I was just taking notice of the pretty dishes. And everything." She was thankful that they could not read her mind and know that she had been thinking, My very first visit in a real house. Stepping inside a kitchen, with baskets to sell, or standing on the front porch, that's not visiting —

The table talk went merrily on. That added to the strangeness of the meal, for Pa didn't want folks to chatter while he ate. "Folks" meant Emmy, since Chad was never a chatterer. Lost in her thoughts, Emmy became aware that Mrs. Carter had asked her a question and was awaiting an answer. "Ma'am?" she faltered.

"Are you liking Miss Marthann's vacation school?"

"Oh, yes, ma'am. I like it a lot."

Phil chuckled. "I don't believe Selby has told the God-in-you story yet."

"Oh, yes, ma'am," Emmy responded quickly. "I mean yes, sir. I mean yes. I didn't quite get the straight of it, though."

"And what's all this?" Mr. Carter asked, helping himself to more chicken and passing the platter.

"Why, you know Miss Selby, how she's a little on the soft side." Phil's voice broke into a high note. "Some time every summer she tells it to the kids. Every time she meets a person who rubs her the wrong way, she always says, 'The God in me salutes the God in you.' "

"Well, what's the idea?" Mr. Carter inquired unbelievingly.

"Why, after that she just has to feel right toward the other guy, don't you see? Can't possibly be mad at God."

Mr. Carter quirked an astonished fair eyebrow at his son. "For Pete's sake, she doesn't say it out loud?"

"Well, no, not even Selby goes that far."

"*Miss* Selby," Mrs. Carter scolded, blinking brown eyes and pushing out reproachful lips toward Phil. "And you make it sound much more outlandish than it is. Miss Selby is a Quaker, too, Emmy. And you know one of the Quaker beliefs is that everybody has a little bit of God within himself."

"That's — kind of nice," Emmy murmured. But astonishing, she thought.

The meal went on with mounting interest through the dessert. Emmy had never before tasted homemade ice cream and angel food.

Finally Mr. Carter rose and stretched his thin length and observed amiably, "Now an old man has the classic right to take a nap with the Denver *Post* and the radio broadcast. Mamma, won't you just this once let the table and the dishes go?"

Emmy spoke with shy eagerness. "Please, can't I help?"

"Aw," moaned Phil in mock despair, "that spills the beans, Emmy. I thought I was going to get out of it slick."

In another five minutes Emmy and Phil and his mother were in the kitchen, making quick, gay work of the dishes. Such a kitchen! Emmy kept thinking. Such dishwashing! No kin to greasy scant suds in a beat-up pan, and tin plates and cups dried on a flour sack and stuck away in a box.

Between times Phil snipped off pieces of cake, or like a conspirator tossed Emmy a brown, delicious half of the one chicken liver that was left.

"Looks as if I couldn't fill you up if I stuffed you like a Strasbourg goose!" Mrs. Carter scolded him lovingly.

Emmy was dizzy with new experiences when at last in late afternoon Phil walked her slowly home. The breeze was blowing gaily. It blew Emmy's curls and she pushed them back with both hands.

"Hi!" said Phil. "There goes your ribbon. I'll put it in my pocket till we get there."

As they entered the clearing they were busily discussing the next week's vacation school, and it was not until Phil had said goodbye and gone whistling down the trail that Emmy focused on the tent and her family.

She stood stock-still, her stomach churning as it had done the few times she rode in an elevator.

Pa said, "Well, get a move on, missy. Don't just stand and gawp."

Emmy moistened her lips. "We — we aren't going now, Pa?"

Pa stared at her. "Yep, tomorrow morning. And why the dickens not? Finished them baskets, and soon as we get the cash from Mis' Jones we're off."

Fury mounted within Emmy until the clearing, bright in the summer sun, shivered into an unreal dazzle before her. It had been months since one of these rages had seized her, and at first she held it down. "Oh, pa, no!" she stammered.

"Oh, missy, yes," Pa retorted.

"Oh, Pa, a few more days? Only a few more days?"

Curtly he shook his head. "Stayed long enough. Too long, I reckon. Don't fancy yore getting too thick with a pretty-pretty mamma's boy like that Carter kid."

"Phil Carter is not a mamma's boy," Emmy blazed. "And he's my friend, just the way Refugio is."

"Oh, yeah?" Pa drawled.

Ma was packing the trunk, just inside the tent, and Emmy whirled toward her. "Ma, I want this so bad. Vacation school. I won't ask for another thing. I won't tease for shoes. Ma, I'll wear this pair all winter, even if my toes stick out. Oh, won't you tell Pa — ?" Seeing Ma's face quiver, Emmy had a moment's wild hope.

But Ma only said, "He's made up his mind."

At the words, Emmy's self-control snapped like a rubber band stretched too tight. The old, wild exhilaration of letting go surged through her. She gritted her teeth and jumped up and down as she had used to do in her little-girl tantrums. "Pa," she gasped through tearing sobs, "Pa, it's — it's hateful of you. I don't care — it's hateful. I'll make you sorry — "

"Emmy!" Ma warned, her eyes blinking worriedly past her daughter.

Emmy whirled around. There stood Phil, his face white.

"This — is yours," he said, holding out her hair ribbon.

Mutely she took it, not looking at him.

"Goodbye, Emmy," he said stiffly.

Again the blood rushed to Emmy's head, and this time her anger lashed out at Phil. "Oh, you think I'm awful." Her voice grated low and passionate. "You think I'm just a no-good heathen and not fitten for you to wipe your shoes on — "

Phil's eyes were bleakly gray.

"Well, let me tell you one thing, Phil Carter. My brother Chad's worth a dozen pretty-pretty mamma's boys who wouldn't say boo to a goose!"

Pricked by her own words, her rage died, going out of her like air out of a toy balloon. Phil was gazing at her solemnly, as if he were someone younger even than Chad. She did not consciously see the defenselessness of his parted lips, as if he were a child who had received an unmerited blow. In the coming years she was to see it a hundred times.

After a silence that stretched long, Phil's lips closed in a firm, straight line, and he turned and went away.

4

Truce

BLINDLY EMMY stumbled across the clearing. Under a low-growing bush she crept, not feeling the sting of the branches that caught at her face and hair.

This couldn't have happened.

She couldn't have killed one of the two friendships which were all she had ever had. Her eyes ached with hot dryness till the tears came, and she cried until she could not breathe. When at last she lay limp and emptied, she heard her mother's voice, close to the bush.

"Emmy. It's the preacher woman."

"Ma," she whimpered, "I can't — "

"You come, Emmy Lou," Ma said.

Ma seldom used that tone. It brought Emmy creeping out. "I must be a sight," she mumbled, catching back a sob as she crouched there and pushed at her hair.

"Go wash yourself," Ma said, with a gesture toward the tent.

The small mirror showed red eyes, swollen lips, tear-stained cheeks. Well, nothing made any difference now. Pulling her rumpled clothes straight, she went slowly out into the open.

Miss Marthann smiled at her as if Emmy were entirely normal. "Emmy," she said briskly, "your mother says you can walk home with me. For once there's nobody there, and we can have a good talk and a bite of supper before I have to go to another meeting."

Emmy choked. "I'd be shamed to my soul if anybody saw me."

"You'll look good as new in no time," Miss Marthann said matter-of-factly. "And we'll lock my front door and if anyone comes we'll make like we aren't there," she added humorously.

Much as Emmy longed to keep her swollen face and difficult breathing at home, she could think of no more excuses. Though she felt as if she and Miss Marthann were walking through crowds of staring people, they actually reached the refuge of the parsonage without meeting anyone.

For a while Miss Marthann talked about trifles, while Emmy sat in one of the cheerfully cushioned chairs she had so wanted to see, staring blindly at her own dusty shoes. She thought afterward that she likely interrupted Miss Marthann in the middle of a sentence. "Miss Marthann, how ever did you know? Did Phil — ?"

Miss Marthann nodded, hazel eyes bright on Emmy.

"Phil wasn't tattling, you understand, Emmy. I've known Phil since he was born, and I guess he couldn't get any farther without letting loose."

"Phil — cried?"

"Doesn't every man that's worth his salt cry sometimes? He thought a lot of you, Emmy. Kind of made a fairy tale around you. Told me more than once — I recollect his very words — 'Such a plucky little kid, Miss Marty. So kind of little and alone and plucky.' And then it hurt his pride, what you said."

Emmy twisted her hands together, unable to speak.

"Perhaps I ought to tell you, Emmy. Ever since he was a baby Phil's been outgrowing a bad case of rheumatic fever. Left a heart weakness. He's had to be careful if he was ever to be strong and sound and able to live the life he's planned. Maybe it's hurt his development in some ways. I suppose it has. But in other ways he's the stronger for it."

Wildly Emmy stared at Miss Marthann, her eyes streaming afresh. "And I taunted him. Oh, I ain't no good," she sobbed, dropping into Pa's manner of speech. "What I says to him — about me — it's all true. I ain't nothing but a heathen kid — what they call a rubber bum — and not fitten. Oh, Miss Marthann, seems like I can't keep aholt of that temper when it gets going. I can't ever amount to nothing. I can't."

"Fiddlesticks. If I were a gambler, I'd bet my wad on you, Emmy Lane."

"Miss Marthann, you're just saying that."

"If you'd known me longer," Miss Marthann said with a dry chuckle, "you'd know I don't butter people up to make them feel good. And as for temper, surely you've seen a young horse showing its teeth and lashing out with its hoofs like a demon. And the same colt when it's trained and all that strength and vim put to good use. Why, it's worth more than a dozen spiritless nags."

"But it's — it's a nasty temper, and I can't — "

"Do you think for a minute that God gave you all that fire and didn't give you the strength to control it?"

Emmy went on shaking her head, and Miss Marthann went on pottering round her plants. "You know usually you kind of like to let go, even if it gets you a licking," she guessed, her long upper lip droll. "But other times, I know, it seems to sweep you off your feet. Dickens had a heroine, Tattycoram, in his *Little Dorrit* I think she is. Someone taught her to count to ten before she said anything when she was mad. I had a friend with a temper like that, and she had another scheme. She'd clasp her hands behind her back and grip them hard. So the nails cut into her palms, sometimes. She said she felt as if Someone was helping her hold on."

"Someone?"

"The Someone who is always with us." Miss Marthann spoke as if she were shy about talking of him.

"I don't know much about such as that," Emmy said hesitantly. "Of course us Lanes believe in God. Seems like you got to believe in God, or who would have made you? But we don't — we don't mention Him."

"Well," Miss Marthann spoke with such energy that neither she nor Emmy noticed the water running from her pitcher over the edge of a flower pot and down on the gay rag carpet, "know what I bet, Emmy Lou Lane? I bet you'll get control of that temper and ride it where you want to go — and where God wants you to go. To school, yes. Seems as if that was the first step."

"And to a house that sits still in one spot?"

Miss Marthann nodded vigorously. "Sure as shooting." She went to the kitchen, to icebox and cupboard, talking through the open door to Emmy. "You know it says in the Bible, 'Ask, and ye shall receive, seek, and ye shall find.' "

"Knock, and the door will come open!" Emmy finished. Again the morning's excitement stirred her. "Miss Marthann, you know what? That's plumb true. Not just preacher's gab — " She flushed at the slip and hurried on, stammering in her eagerness. "It works, Miss Marthann. But I've sure had to give some of the doors a shove myself."

"How right you are!" Miss Marthann agreed, nodding double and triple nods above the trays she was bringing in, her long upper lip folded down over the lower, eyes blinking reminiscently. "But go on, Emmy. Tell me some more. Sounds as if you'd been having experiences."

"Oh, yes, ma'am. Yes, ma'am, that's how everything

began to change. For me. Ever since Phil brought me that book and I plumb had to learn to read it. Well, and ever since Abbie Allen's birthday party. I thought right then, them kids — those children — they're clean and smooth and have houses that stay put. And why? Well, one thing's sure, they all go to school. So the very next place we set up the tent was right next door to a schoolhouse. Awful lucky it happened so. So I — I knocked at the door, like the preacher said, and that's how everything got started."

She looked down at the tray she had been holding unregarded on her knees, and took a bite of the buttered bread, suddenly self-conscious.

"Goodness," Miss Marthann objected, "do go on with the story. This I want to hear."

Emmy swallowed her bite convulsively and waved the rest of the slice in emphasis. "Pa and Ma thought Chad and me was swinging and sliding in the school yard while the kids was inside. I'd given myself a sort of cat-lick in the washbasin at home when nobody was looking, but — A big boy in the hall asked me what I thought I was doing there, and stared at me like I was going to walk off with anything that was lying round loose. Not much wonder, the way I looked. So I managed to ask him where the little kids went to school, and he pointed to a door. I guess I'd have run away if he hadn't been watching me. But I had to knock, and, Miss Marthann, it was Miss Mary that opened the door."

LIVINGSTONE COLLEGE
SALISBURY, N. C. 28144

Emmy took a deep breath and seemed to catch again the fragrance that was Miss Mary and the shine of her eyes when Emmy said, "Can I come to your school, ma'am? Can I, please?" "And me looking like something the cat drug in — dragged in," Emmy said wonderingly aloud, and then flushed deeply, thinking of ears and fingernails. It had been so long before Emmy realized fingernails, and so much longer before she thought anything about ears.

"Seemed like everything was lucky for me," she went on thoughtfully. "First Chad was bad sick with the measles, so we had to stay there nigh on to a month — nearly a month. And with Miss Mary just an angel from heaven, no kid could keep from learning a lot, even if she hadn't had to — just plumb had to — get to reading and writing quick — The supper is real nice and tasty, Miss Marthann, ma'am."

"And so you went on knocking. Mind if I tell Phil?"

"No, ma'am," Emmy murmured, when she could swallow the cold meat in her mouth. "I kept on knocking, you might say. Sometimes it looked like it wasn't going to work. But it did. Course it was a help to keep thinking, There's a law in this country, says kids got to go to school. Must work the other way, too: schools got to take the kids when they come. But it shows the verse is true, don't it? All kinds of teachers and all kinds of schools, and even when we wouldn't be there but two-three days, every last one let me in." Emmy's voice trailed off wonderingly.

"Those eyes!" Miss Marthann commented. "And you wanting it with every little inch of you! And schoolteachers — well, I've found them pretty fine myself."

When supper was over, Emmy went home half happy. Only half. There remained the fact that Phil had witnessed her tantrum.

Next morning the Lanes were stowing things away in the truck. They made quick work of it, after all their years of roving. Pa wouldn't have cared about things being in order, except that he didn't want any bother about getting them out next time. So the tent was folded into a tight bundle, and the weary old mattresses were laid out in the truck body, two deep — "So a fellow could stretch out for a nap in the daytime, and easy pull them out to make beds for the nights when they didn't stop to pitch tent, which was most nights," he would say.

Pa had a couple of poles rigged up at the front and back of the truck between which a line could be stretched across and the tarp hung like a tent for rainy nights when they wanted to sleep there. It didn't rain so often in that part of the country, though. The quilts were folded in a pile to one side, with the tarp over them, when they were traveling. Kettles and skillets and pie tins and the like went into a box, and the family clothes into the trunk. Once Pa had tried to show Ma how they could get more into the trunk if the kids got in and stamped things down, but Ma wouldn't hear of it. That was because she had a little red plush box right next to the Good Book, and she was afraid it would get hurt. It had a brooch of her mother's, and some other little trinkets, even a blue glass slipper that was Ma's grandmother's. Finally, a special place under the seat was kept for the old bird cage that plagued Pa so.

Emmy had long hated the confusion, and the gritty feeling of the quilts and their stale smell over her at night, but never so sharply as now, after being in the parsonage and in the Carter house. If Ma had ever lived like that, anywhere near like that, how could she put up with this?

Emmy tried to think back how it was when she could first remember. Seems like they had had sheets and pillowcases then, and Ma had spent a heap of time washing whenever they stopped where there was enough water. Emmy didn't know exactly when things had changed. Little by little, probably. Ma wasn't too well, and she lost the get-up and go to fight the disorder and dirt of the wandering life. As she thought about it, Emmy shook out an old comfort so fiercely that another bunch of cotton wadding flew out of its ragged end.

For several years now Emmy had contrived to wash jeans and shirts for herself and Chad, pulling them out straight with her hands while they were drying, and they looked almost ironed. She couldn't force Chad to wear underclothes, but while they were in school she nagged him till he kept his face and hands washed. Even these personal changes had cost Emmy ingenuity and hard work. They had not extended to living conditions, and now it seemed to Emmy that she could stand no more of the dirt and disorder.

When Phil's hoo-hoo sounded from the clearing entrance, she flung the comfort into the truck bed and hurried to meet him, so that he should not come far enough to see the confusion. She was sure he had stopped there in order to warn her, in case she should be having another tantrum, but even though that was the reason, she was thankful that he had come no nearer.

"Miss Marthann says you're really going," Phil said soberly. "I had to tell you goodbye. And how's about writing to me again, huh? I'll answer whenever you give me an address to send to."

He was studying her gravely, his fair face flushed.

Achingly Emmy longed to take back the hateful things she had said about him, but she could not think how, especially with Chad staring under black brows. "Phil," she stammered, "I'm — I'm awful sorry." She stooped to pat the curly black dog, so that Phil should not see her wet lashes.

Phil cleared his throat. "Well, goodbye. Take care of yourself. Goodbye, Mrs. Lane. Goodbye, Mr. Lane. I hope you have a nice trip. So long, kid," he said to Chad. "So long, Emmy."

When he was gone, Pa straightened up and growled, "Said he was a sissy and I got no reason to change my mind. Ketch me talking mealymouthed to folks who blew our top about him like we did yesterday. Sissy."

Emmy swallowed a lump in her throat and did not try to answer.

5

Magic—Assorted Varieties

THE LANE truck clattered northward through Denver and approached Fort Lupton, with Emmy increasingly eager. The Luceros were usually there at this time of year, staying on from beets to green peas, and then to fall activities in the beets again. Emmy had never been quite so eager to see Refugio. Ma had withdrawn into a vagueness deeper than customary, and Refugio was the only one to whom Emmy could tell all that had happened: about vacation school, that is, and Sunday dinner at the Carters', and supper at the parsonage. Even to Refugio she could not reveal the sordid story of her tantrum, of what in her own mind, she already called That Day.

"S'pose we're hiring out in the peas," Emmy said when they came in sight of the town.

Pa shifted his tobacco to the other cheek, blue-black with stubble, spat sidewise, shook his head.

"Pa! What you mean?"

"Not stopping for no crops this time. Stopped too long

back yonder." And see what it got us, his tone seemed to add.

Emmy stared unbelieving. "Pa, you don't mean it?"

"Yep." Pa didn't even look at her.

His indifference sent a rush of fury to Emmy's brain, the familiar tingle up her spine. "Pa," she began to stutter. With a mighty effort she stopped, gripping her hands behind her, though the truck seat was a poor place for the gesture. Her rage went on boiling. What was it Miss Selby said when she didn't like folks? Right now Emmy sure didn't like Pa.

She tightened her lips and silently repeated it over and over: "The God in me salutes the God in you — if there is any of God in you, Pa, which I doubt," she added. Her hands were clenched till they ached, and she glared at her father, stretching out her neck till her fluff of curls brushed his cheek.

"Gosh all fishhooks!" he protested, shifting in his seat. "What the dickens is eating you, girl? Sure do give a fellow the willies, grinding yore teeth and scowling like that. No way for a youngun to act to her pa. Spit it out, missy, and be done with it."

Emmy relaxed. This was an unexpected by-product. Maybe Miss Marthann wouldn't approve, but it was certainly a satisfaction, to keep from blowing her top and get Pa's goat at the same time.

That night when, well to the north of Fort Lupton, the Lanes had settled themselves to sleep in the truck, the humor of the event struck Emmy. For a long time she lay laughing to herself, but quietly, not to waken the family. It made her forget a little the stale smells, the grittiness, the lumpiness of the mattress. Forgetting had grown more difficult since the stop at Glen Lake.

She had need of laughter. Pa tried her control many times in the next months, and she had to put her new incantations to work repeatedly.

Once when they stopped for a few days at the edge of a town, Emmy hunted up the library, and learned that she could read books on the premises, though she could not take them out. With shy pride she asked for *Little Dorrit*, by Dickens. She remembered the author, though previously she had supposed the name was only a mild swear word. Besides, she had a quick and tenacious memory. Pa said it was because she hadn't cluttered it up with all this book and radio rubbish.

Little Dorrit proved slow reading, with its solid pages of fine print. Emmy skipped over description and philosophy to get to the folks and the story. She read intensely, sitting with elbows on table, chin in hands, curls falling over her face. Lost in this new world, she read till closing time, when the librarian had to come and touch her on the shoulder. Emmy lifted blind eyes, unable to pull herself back into the reality of the small Nevada town.

"I'm sorry the rules won't let you take it out," the librarian said. "But come earlier tomorrow."

"Thank you, ma'am." Emmy went out, still a part of

the strange story. Amazing that there should be worlds so unknown and undreamed! Debtors' prisons would be worse even than the roving life of the Lanes. How ever can I wait till tomorrow? she asked herself. I haven't even come to the girl with the odd-turned name and the tantrums.

Chad was waiting for her a little way from the tent. "Gosh, didn't even sell your baskets. You're going to ketch it," he warned in his slow, deep voice. He often resented Emmy, but he didn't want anyone else to be cross to her, not even Pa.

Spasmodically Emmy quickened her step. "Because I've been gone so long?"

"Yeah. Pa's fit to be tied."

That time Pa didn't say much. His glare froze the family to silence as they ate supper, though Emmy did murmur to Ma, "I found an awful good book at the library. Miss Marthann told me the name of it. Ma, I'm sorry about not getting home to help, but the time just flew."

While she washed the dishes, using more hot water and more soap then she used to, she told Chad some of the story. He lay on his back on the ground, seeing how far his feet would walk up the side of the tent. He didn't look as if he were listening, but when they went to bed, with his pallet next to hers, he mumbled, "Listen, Emmy. If you talked quiet, so's not to rile Pa?"

Emmy tried going on with the story, but Pa soon sat up and roared at her. "Work all day while yore young one sits around, and then be kept awake all night while she hashes over a fool storybook without a word of truth in it! Come morning we're starting on, missy, so you'll get to sleep if you know what's good for you."

Emmy lay still as a mouse. If Pa went straight off to sleep he might forget what he'd said. But when she woke next morning he was vigorously banging around, and she could see the signs of a prompt move.

"Ma," she complained, "it's just plain contrary of Pa. Pitched tent and all and said we would stay the balance of the week."

Ma was making corn pone, dripping corn-meal batter into bacon fat that sizzled over the fire. "Men — he sets store by you young ones, but — he — he wants to keep things like they are — "

"How can I stand it to go off without finding out how Little Dorrit makes it, and that odd-named one?" Emmy grumbled, holding the tin plates for Ma to dish the pone into as soon as she flipped it over and let it crisp on the other side. "S'pose I've got to leave them hanging that way all the rest of my life?"

Sometimes Ma surprised Emmy by coming out of the clouds. This morning her common-sense tone resembled Miss Marthann's, though without the chuckle. "Most towns got libraries. Most libraries got Dickens."

Ma proved right. In another Nevada town and again in California Emmy located libraries and snatched bits of the novel.

In that California library a piece of rich good luck befell her. As often before, she read until a bell blared sharply. Looking up, dazed, she saw that the last readers were straggling out. She herself got up and stumbled to the desk, reading, laid the book on the desk, and leaned over it for one last line.

The librarian laughed a little rippling laugh at Emmy's absorption. She was a little, brown, rippling librarian, not so tall as Emmy. She smelled something like Miss Mary, Emmy's first teacher.

"Maybe you can finish it tomorrow. No, it will take longer than that," she corrected herself, looking at the number of the page.

"Oh, my," Emmy said resignedly. "We're going on tomorrow morning, soon as ever we've et — eaten."

Contemplating Emmy, the little brown librarian nibbled one lip. "Look," she said, "when books are just about so old and worn, we have to get rid of them. I seem to remember a discarded copy of *Little Dorrit*. If you'd care for it."

She led the way to a room that was musty with old books. A wonderful room, Emmy thought, shut off from the world and solid with books from floor to ceiling. The librarian squatted, childlike, to peer along a low shelf, cried "Goody!" and pulled out a book that she handed up to Emmy, smiling. "Make sure it's all there," she advised, and turned to look further. *Little Dorrit* was intact, and Emmy joyfully took it home, along with *The Old Curiosity Shop* and *David Copperfield*.

"Mine to keep forever!" she told Chad.

"If Paw don't heave 'em out," Chad warned her.

The Lanes worked in the crops all that summer. Emmy was unusually industrious, and for a reason. When fall came, she would beg Pa to go to Glen Lake, so that she could start in the Consolidated School at Obelisk, four miles away. Phil had told her what a good school it was. He would be in high school there, and so would Abbie. Emmy refused to call her Gail, even in her thoughts. Gail! The strange and fancy name seemed to give Abbie an unfair advantage.

Emmy found a little time to read during the long summer evenings, lengthened still more by daylight saving time. She tried reading aloud to Chad, but he was bored and wanted to wander around and see things. What he did like was to have her retell the stories while they were riding in the back of the truck.

Once that fall, when they had sold all their baskets and had a spare hour, she tried to lure her brother into a library with her. "But you ought to have seen that boy," she told her mother. "Walled his eyes like a balky horse and waited for me outside. About books he's Pa all over again."

"You took after me. About books," Ma said in her halting way.

"Did you love to read?" Emmy demanded incredulously.

Ma nodded.

But not like me, Emmy thought. She could not put into words what books were to her. They opened treasure strange, rich, and varied that she had never known existed. They let her escape from the dusty drabness of her life to explore fine houses and palaces and exotic lands. Best of all, they let her into quiet little houses with bookcases and pianos, houses she could never have. Never.

She made one attempt to express her feelings to Ma. "You go into a liberry — librar-y — full of books from the floor to the roof and up the middle, and every blame' book jam-packed with new things — all yours to read. And there's something about its being so quiet, with all kinds of folks reading at the tables — and the — the smell of books — "

And there was never any telling what you might stumble on, she thought. Once it was a book about Okies, getting starved out, and run out by farming machinery, in the dust-bowl days she had heard Pa talk of. Emmy read in that book for an hour, repelled and fascinated. It was like the life she knew, dusty and grimy and uncomely, she thought, and not fitten to put into a book. A few times when they had eaten at a campfire in a hobo jungle, Emmy had seen acts and heard words that were here set down in print. After the first fascinated and repelled hour she did not read more. It was no treat to her.

Another time she happened on an ancient leather-bound volume of cures, which a reader had left open on a table. Looking through it, Emmy thought if she could find an old-fashioned remedy for her mother's ills, Pa might not be so set against it as he was against doctors and drugstores. All this summer Ma had been headachy, and so dizzy that she had to catch hold of things when she started to walk.

Emmy found numerous promising prescriptions and made a painstaking list of the plants mentioned: gentian, chicory, shepherd's purse, valerian, eucalyptus. Pa would know most of them and where to find them. Emmy herself knew some, such as the shepherd's purse which Ma often had her gather as a tonic for Pet, her canary.

Pa did hunt up several of the herbs, and gruffly ordered Ma to give them a trial. Yet, as autumn approached, she grew no better.

Staying there in San Diego County for some weeks to work in the celery, Emmy found other matters more interesting even than the book of herbs. She found a good school, and she received letters from Phil and Miss Marthann.

Both Pa and Chad glowered at Phil's letter. Chad slouched against the tent, flicking disgusted glances at Emmy as she read and chuckled. Pa was stretched on the ground to rest after a hot day of weeding that had drenched them all with the smell of celery. His ragged old hat was pulled down over his face, but Emmy could feel

his eyes watching her from beneath it.

"Don't you get no ideas, missy," he growled. "That's all I got to say: don't you get no ideas."

Impatiently Emmy tossed her head. "Pa, I'm fifteen, and so's Phil, and we're just good friends. Phil and Refugio are my best friends and I'm theirs." She hadn't meant to say that, and she knew it was a mistake as soon as the words left her lips.

"Oh, yeah?" Chad drawled in his deep voice. "Ask that Abbie, or Gail, whichever she is. Boy told me her and Phil was going steady."

"Charles Lane Junior, you just made that up."

"I never either," Chad indignantly denied.

"Ought to know Chad don't story," Pa grunted.

That was too true, Emmy thought desolately. And it was no wonder Phil liked Abbie, so smooth and ladylike, and so softly pretty. Phil would never catch Abbie stamping and yelling in a tantrum.

As if her thoughts were not already painful enough, the bulky envelope from Miss Marthann sharpened the hurt. Miss Marthann's personal letter reflected, though dimly, the warmth of its writer, and was far from inflicting wounds. Miss Marthann had hoped Emmy could get home in time to start the year at Obelisk with the Glen young folks, but maybe next year she could go on with them. She said she would enclose one of the mimeographed letters she sent out to the summer people who were interested in the Little Log Church, and to the boys scattered far and wide in the armed forces. And she was hoping there might be work at the Glen next summer that would specially suit Pa, but more of that later.

Emmy reread that last sentence aloud. "What you reckon she's got up her sleeve now?" she mused.

Ma was leaning against a tent pole and staring at the

horizon. Impatiently Emmy thought that Ma never liked being where she was, these days.

Now Ma shook her head. "We couldn't — your pa — "

Pa grunted agreement with the half-spoken idea.

"Oh, Ma!" Emmy protested longingly.

She turned to the mimeographed letter and skimmed through it for familiar names till she came to a paragraph that halted her.

> Our young people entertained parents and friends with a play in the Town Hall. Glen Lake turned out handsomely, and the affair netted $30 for the church building fund. Supporting parts were well presented, and the two leads brought down the house. These were the young husband and wife, played convincingly by Phil Carter and Gail Allen.

Emmy wadded the paper with violent fingers and hurled it into the fire. "Pa," she said in a tremulous voice, "don't you think Ma might feel better if we were to settle down somewhere for a spell?"

Pa shoved his hat back from his face and shot her a keen glance. "No place special, I suppose?"

Emmy at first missed the sarcasm in his tone. "Well, maybe Glen Lake. Since we got ground there where we can stop as long as we please. Then I could go to the high school at Obelisk."

Pa raised his long body with a jerk, and his glare intensified. "What's got into you, Emmy Lane? Think yore ma's likely to feel better stuck up there in the snow and ice? And when did you ever hear her hanker after Glen Lake and them narrow-minded hidebound biddies? Young ones is sure selfish. You want schooling so bad you'd walk over yore ma to get it."

Ma murmured, "The snow — there isn't so much as you think — "

"Now don't you give in to everything yore kids take a shine to," Pa adjured her. "If Emmy's so sharp-set for schooling she'll get it someway. Like Old Abe. She hain't got to drag the whole family to the Ar'tic Circle after it."

"I don't know — if I could see a doctor — " Ma put in.

"Sure. And there's never been hide or hair of a doctor at Glen Lake." Pa spoke as if he were at war with Emmy and had won a skirmish. "Tell you what, Ma. Remember that camp near Riverside? Name of Conchita? They always got a good doctor there. He treated Chad for ringworm once. Now I don't hold no more with doctors than I always did, but if you want we can settle down there for the winter and give him a try. It ain't peak harvest yet, but I hear they're short of lemon pickers, and we're good hands with the lemons. Or there's harvesting zinnia seeds or thinning lettuce. Only it seems like we've about had our fill of stoop jobs." Unconsciously Pa rubbed his back.

Emmy loosed a sigh of exasperation that brought Pa's eyes to her face again.

"Now look, missy. Wasn't it you who set such store

by the showers they got at that camp? And the toilets and laundry?"

Emmy breathed hard. "I only thought if Ma — "

"If you're so fretted about yore ma, what's to hinder yore taking over and giving her a real rest? You're growed enough to do a woman's work."

At that Ma roused herself to protest. "Pa, she does the washing. And the dishes. And crops and school too — "

The whole of Emmy, from the center out, was quivering with sick fear and shock. She tried hopelessly to steady her voice. "Yes, Pa, it does seem like I couldn't do much more. Not and keep up in second year of high school — "

Pa said, "Then you can just count school out. Rest of this year, anyway." He stared at her under his black brows as if expecting one of her old rages.

Right now there was in Emmy nothing so strong and vital as rage. Cold and hopeless, she sat and stared at the ground without even thinking. When, gradually, thoughts did come, they were not happy ones. *Emmy Lane, you've been a plain fool. A person is what she is. Belongs with her own kind. Can't get away from what she's born to. Can't get away.*

Pa went away in the truck, came back, scowled at Emmy, who sat where he had left her, hands loose in her lap. Silently he tossed her the latest number of the small magazine that still sold for a nickel in some of the grocery stores. Mechanically Emmy opened it, not thanking Pa, because she didn't feel thankful. Still mechanically, she leafed through the gay pages and paused out of habit at the department titled "Teen Scene." Large letters inquired, "SHOULD SIXTEEN-YEAR-OLDS GO STEADY?" Well, whether they should or not, the sore spot in Emmy's chest assured her that Phil and Abbie probably did. If it were anyone except that hateful, smug Abbie. Not that Emmy gave a hang about Phil Carter or any other boy. But she felt left out and alone.

Emmy would always feel left out and alone. That was what everything added up to.

6

Andrés

THE NEXT MONTHS were hard ones.

At Conchita the camp doctor looked Ma over and said she was a really sick woman — sick in mind and body. He gave her pills and told her to rest and to eat good, strengthening food, meat and fruit and vegetables. Sometimes, he told Pa, the mind righted itself when the body did. He took no notice of Emmy, who felt sick herself. Now it was Emmy who resembled her childhood doll before Pa replaced its worn-out elastic. All Emmy's joints felt loose, and there was a weight on her chest so that she couldn't seem to breathe deep.

Mechanically she worked in the lemon grove that day. Mechanically she got supper, mostly out of cans, and washed up afterward. One thing was true: it was easier to wash dishes in one of these shacks that was provided for the migratory workers than it was over a campfire.

In school Emmy had heard about the importance of dishwashing, and in the grocery magazine, too, but the lessons and the articles seemed not to apply to her. Since her experience in helping wash up in the Carter kitchen Emmy's notions had changed. Now it was hot water. Plenty of soap. Clean dish towels.

The clean dish towels were hard to achieve, even in a shack like this one.

"Pa," Emmy said tonight, her voice snapping out of control, "that's a dish towel you're using."

Pa scowled down at the grayish flour sack with which he had been wiping off his fishpole, scowled up at Emmy. "Look here, missy," he snapped back, "you're getting a little bit too finicky these days. How's a nice clean fishpole going to hurt yore old dishrag?" He glared again, and added, "Kind of fretty you've been lately, too. What ails you? I take notice you don't git no more letters from the Glen."

"I didn't give anyone this address," Emmy said tonelessly.

It was pride, she supposed, that had kept her from sending the address even to Miss Marthann. Phil hadn't answered the letter she wrote just before they came to Conchita. If he were to change his mind about writing, and ask Miss Marthann, he'd see that Emmy didn't care much about hearing from him.

She hadn't realized how much she had counted on their letters. Doing without them was like eating potatoes without salt. But she might just as well get used to it, she told herself harshly. If she'd never got those foolish ideas in the first place, she'd be as contented as the girls around her, not knowing that there was any life better than this aimless one. Nothing better than banging from place to place in an old truck, working hard all day to get enough to eat so that you could work hard the next day to get enough to eat —

Chad was the only one of the Lanes who seemed no different from usual, though it was true you could never be certain what he was thinking, he was so silent. He worked well for a boy of thirteen. Like Pa, he had clever hands, strong and delicate in their touch. Even when he was ten Pa had taught him to handle the clippers so as to cut the citrus stems just right, neither too long, so that they bruised the other fruit, nor so short that they were bruised by the clippers. He had taught him how to drop the fruit into the picking bag quickly but gently; how to hold the filled bag over the basket and trip the cord that ran through rings around the bottom of the bag, so that the bottom opened and let the waxy pale yellow ovals out. He could do it all as well as Emmy could.

Though undersized, Chad was built like Pa, his lean body tough. When he wasn't working, he was prowling round, or helping Pa tinker the truck, or lying on his stomach reading space stories or Superman in the comic books. He didn't get into trouble like many of the boys in camp, but sometimes Emmy would come out of herself long enough to look at her brother with eyes that saw him. When she did, she ached with pity for him, for he, too, was missing school and all that school gave. Once, watching his complete absorption in the doings of Flash Gordon, she paused to tousle his head and say, "Poor old Chaddie, you never did get to read well enough to tackle anything better than comics, did you?"

Chad squirmed away from her hand. "Leave me be," he growled. "Comics is okay."

It was when the family seemed at its lowest ebb that a new outfit pulled into camp one evening, ready to start work the next day. The outfit was the Luceros'.

The Lucero car was a better one than formerly, and it pulled a trailer filled with supplies. Seeing Refugio, Emmy's spirits lifted. She had been thinking of her often, pairing her as she did with her one other friend, Phil Carter.

Refugio was prettier than ever, from her pert haircut and big, shining dark eyes to the toes of her fancy shoes. Emmy was dubious about the dark red polish on Refugio's long oval nails, but noticed that the knuckles were several shades lighter than they used to be.

When she saw Emmy, Refugio shrieked her delighted amazement. "You've sure grown up! I mean you really have," she crowed, grasping Emmy's shoulders and pretending she had to stand on tiptoe to kiss her.

Emmy hid her own emotion with a laugh, the Spanish volatility embarrassing her. "I can't say you've grown, Refugio. When did you get so little? You going to be a runt all your life?"

"Runt, I like that. I think I'm a pretty nice size right now. Hope I don't grow no more. I'm seventeen, almost eighteen, you know that? It's okay on you, though, to be so tall," she added consolingly. "You'd be real pretty if you took a little pains, Emmy, you know that?"

"Don't let her fool you, kid," a masculine voice drawled. "Know what? You're plenty easy on the eyes like you are."

Startled, Emmy peered over Refugio's curled head into the eyes of Refugio's next brother, who had come up silently behind her. "Why, Andrés," she stammered, "I didn't notice you — "

Andrés managed to swagger and droop, look admiring and reproachful, all at the same time. "Fine thing to tell a fellow." he complained. His eyes were on a level with her own, and they were like Refugio's, dark and lustrous as ripe chokecherries. They were exciting eyes, and lifted Emmy's spirits still higher.

He is just as handsome as anybody; maybe handsomer, she thought. And, as Pa says, what's schooling, anyhow? It just makes folks like us discontented.

The Lucero family showed no discontent. Like a flock of gay birds they fluttered round the Lanes with laughing outcry. Mrs. Lucero had grown fatter, but the shining black waves and curls of her new permanent showed not a thread of gray. Her newest baby sat astride her hip, bouncing and blowing bubbles. "And is sure okay, no?" Mrs. Lucero gurgled.

Luckily a shack next to the Lanes' had just been vacated, and the Luceros were allowed to take possession of it. Long after Ma and Chad and Emmy had settled down on their pallets, their neighbors continued to laugh and chatter and bang. Pa had stayed outside to smoke a pipe with Mr. Lucero, whom he admitted to be a "plumb white Mex." The Luceros were the only "furriners" Pa would tolerate.

Someone was plucking a guitar and singing, and Emmy caught the words of a song which had been popular a few years earlier. "Sappy song," she muttered. Softly it stole through the shack door: "And she sighed as she whispered,

'*Mañana!*' Never dreaming that we were parting. And I lied as I — "

"Serenading?" Ma asked in the dimness.

"Oh, no!" Emmy sat up indignantly and then flounced down on her bed again. "Well, if Andrés thinks I'm interested in anything like that, he's got another think coming."

Yet she was smiling as she drifted off to sleep. Andrés was nice-looking and decent. And admiration and appreciation were as comforting as a warm fire on a chilly day.

The work at camp did not seem so hard after the Luceros came. Their noise, their laughter, their singing, and even their occasional shrieking quarrels blew away some of the stagnant dullness that had settled down on Emmy.

The young Luceros were enthusiastic attendants at the numerous evening classes and entertainments open to them at the Center, and they tried to get Emmy and Chad to go with them. "They even got a Spanish troop of Girl Scouts," Refugio's next sister, Margarita, told Emmy. "You ain't too old, Emmy, and it's sure fun. Oh, I always do forget you're Anglo."

Pa was still adamant in his refusal to let his daughter and son join the classes. The Lanes were not migratory workers, he reminded them, and he wasn't going to let them be labeled as such when they merely worked in the crops as it suited their own convenience. Trash, most of the migrants were, he accused.

One gentle Friday evening, however, Refugio coaxed

Emmy to accompany her when she took some flowers to Miss Kay, one of the missionary workers.

"I'm going with Refugio," Emmy told Ma. "It's not a party or a class or a meeting, so Pa's got no call to say I didn't mind him."

Andrés loped lithely after the girls, and strolled along at Emmy's side. It was a pity he wasn't fair-haired. Emmy could not seem to take a fancy to a dark-haired boy. And though the admiration in his eyes might give her a lift, it also made her feel uncomfortably warm and crowded, as if she were riding in a full bus. She liked space and fresh air.

Refugio chattered insouciantly, an occasional Spanish word erupting from her slangy English. "You'll sure be surprise', Emmy. Won't she be knock' for a loop, Andrés? Miss Kay and her *amiga*, they ask for this old empty garage. Hadn't been used for years, so the foreman say, *Ciertamente*, okay, go as far as they want. And you wouldn't never believe it. They didn't spend no money, hardly, but it looks real good. Funny, kind of, but good."

They were approaching the garage, which Emmy remembered from past years. Even the outside was changed. Morning-glory vines mantled it with green, the heavenly blue blossoms now twisted shut and the pleated buds awaiting the dawn. The small fenced yard sported grass and other flowers. From the door hung a sign, THE BEE-HIVE.

Still chattering, Refugio banged the little iron knocker.

"She's sure smart, Miss Kay. She ask' for a piece of pine wood from the scrap heap: one with knotholes, she says, and the foreman let her pick through the pile, and — oh, *buenas tardes*, Miss Kay. Meet my friend Emmy Lane. She's been my girl friend ever since I can remember. I was just telling her how you burnt the name on — " she jerked a finger toward the sign — "and then finished it off with the shiny stuff. Nice as if it was boughten."

Curiously Emmy looked around her when they had gone inside. Here staring was good manners, because Miss Kay liked to have them stare. With bubbling laughter she was telling Emmy and Andrés about making that interior. Refugio listened with the superior smile of one who knows all about it, occasionally putting in a word for explanation or emphasis.

"Those bunk beds you see through the door — we built them ourselves, out of four-by-fours and two-by-fours. All we had to buy were springs and mattresses. Don't you love our bright blue paint?"

"Real Mexican blue." Refugio patronized the color.

"On'y thing," Andrés said, regarding the glossy surfaces, "they'd ought to have some nice bright flowers painted on them someplace."

"You're nominated. Will you do it, Andrés?" Miss Kay challenged. "They could match those cretonne curtains that make our clothes closets."

Emmy was interestedly eying the curtain partitions between bedroom and living-dining room. She touched them with a deferential finger. "Weren't these awfully expensive?"

"They wouldn't be in our house if they were expensive," Miss Kay disclaimed, laughing. "We got the bamboo shade cut the right size and then put tape across the edge to sew rings to. When you push them back — look! they fold on the pole in nice, tidy pleats. We haven't decided whether to leave them natural color or paint them."

"Red!" Refugio observed explosively. "Same as the little stand and your eating table."

"The tables are pretty," Emmy admired. "And so clean and smooth."

"We made the little one, and bought the other at a secondhand store. Only things we spent any real money for were these easy chairs. We got them secondhand, too, and slip-covered them ourselves. Stretching out in a soft chair at the end of a busy day and listening to the radio — even a few minutes is good medicine.

"Wish I could offer you something to munch or drink," she interrupted herself. "Right now we're cleaned out. Those kids! Maybe you'd like a glass of ice water, though." Proudly she motioned toward an electric refrigerator. "Brand-new. My folks sent the money for it."

Ice water, coolly clinking and covering the outside of the glasses with a chilly mist, was one of the wonderful things people took for granted, Emmy thought, as she sipped hers, looking around to fix details in mind. Low bookcases across this room divided it from the kitchen part, and held a few books and magazines, the radio, and a bowl of wild flowers.

"Did you catch on to how the bookcases was fixed, Emmy?" Refugio asked as if she had made them.

"I saw them like that in the grocery magazine, but I never thought they'd look so good."

Stacks of red-painted bricks formed the ends and supported the pine-plank shelves.

"Emmy's a great one for reading," Refugio told Miss Kay. "You can bet she'd notice your bookcases. Me, I can read good, of course. Learned here at the Center. But I sure ain't nuts about it, like Emmy." She was exhibiting her friend to Miss Kay, even as she had exhibited Miss Kay's apartment to her friend.

"But Emmy's okay, all the same," Andrés put in.

"Like to borrow some reading matter, Emmy?" Miss Kay asked. "Here's a book we just managed to finish. I think you'd like it. We did." She took a volume from the shelf, leafed through, smiling at the pages as if they were personal friends, and handed the book to Emmy.

Hungry for books though she was, Emmy took this one reluctantly. She had cut loose from that world. "I don't know if I ought to — "

Miss Kay pressed the book upon her. "Oh, you'll find time. Just so you get it back before you go on."

They sauntered home, past a few solid company houses, past the laundry building and the bathhouse, past shacks and a scattering of tents. The California air was fragrant with trees; eucalyptus and pepper, Ma said they were. The moon was coming up, huge and misty-red and etched with a drooping pepper branch.

"They sure fixed up their place nice," Emmy murmured.

"Neat." As if remembering, Refugio giggled. "Miss Kay says she didn't ask the church folks for furniture. On purpose she didn't. Says they'd have sent a lot, but no two pieces would have looked good together. So she waited till she and Miss Amy had it most done, and then she just ask' straight out for cretonnes like in Monkey Ward or maybe Sawbuck, and for money to buy the bamboo shade and the paint."

"Refugio," Emmy asked, "don't you ever hanker to quit drifting and settle down? Most anybody could find enough money to fix up a little place like that," she added yearningly.

"Gosh, I never thought. Seems like settling down would be awful dull. *Después de todo,* camps like this are more fun, seems like."

"This isn't so bad," Emmy admitted, "but how many of them have showers and washing places and hot and cold water? And even here no water in the house and no screens. And is there anything duller than forever banging around the country in a truck? Everything the same, over and over and over." Involuntarily she looked at Andrés for support, and found him gazing at the moon, his handsome face sober. "You see what I mean, Andrés?"

"I dunno, Emmy. I always liked this okay. Things going on; new places; new folks. Maybe I'd want it different when I got married." A moment's blank silence followed the word. "I never thought much about it." Andrés himself sounded surprised by what he had said. "But when a man's nineteen — Emmy, we could fix up a place like that — " He tossed a backward gesture toward the remodeled garage.

"Where'd be the room for ten people?" Emmy scoffed.

"I meant — you and me."

Emmy's mouth dropped open with the impact of his words. She swallowed and moved closer to Refugio, away from Andrés.

Refugio giggled uncontrollably, clutching at her own slim waist, before she could bring out a warning. "Andrés, behave! Emmy's two years younger'n me. She's too young to get married."

"Gee, Emmy, I thought you was more'n sixteen." Andrés sounded surprised and regretful. "But all the same there's lots of girls get hitched when they're sixteen," he added thoughtfully.

"Not me, Andrés. And Pa would blow his top if I so much as thought of it."

"Well," Andrés agreed, "I'm not in any big rush. I'd wait till you was seventeen. If I had your word."

Emmy's curls flew from side to side with her vigorous headshake. "Oh, no, Andrés. I haven't ever thought of you that way. And I'd rather be — be just a girl a long time yet."

"Well, you think about me now," Andrés ordered her. "Honest, Emmy, you could do worse. I can work as steady as the next one, especially if I got a reason to."

"Oh, hush," his sister bade him, squeezing Emmy's arm. "You give her time. Look. We might have us a double date tomorrow night. How's it strike you, Andrés? Emmy?"

"Double date?" Emmy repeated.

Refugio rolled roguish eyes. "You just wait till you see my new boy friend. But Papa and Mamma, they're so old-fashioned they won't let me date unless Andrés or Joe goes along."

"And a good thing they won't," Andrés scolded. "I ain't too hot about this last kid, Refugio. What do you know about him, anyway?"

"Have I got to meet all his folks, Andrés? Fat lot of dates there'd be if a girl had to do that. All I know is his folks have broke up and he's on his own. With an allowance. And a car. And him an Anglo," she added in triumph.

When Emmy went in that night Pa and Ma and Chad were all quiet on their mattresses on the floor. Emmy undressed cautiously, not to wake them and invite questions. For a long time she lay thinking about Andrés, and trying to feel as girls seemed to feel in stories. It ought to be a thrilling event, the first proposal, and from a boy as good-looking as a movie star. It oughtn't to be flat like this.

She pulled her mind away from Andrés to the garage which Miss Kay and her co-worker had made into a home. Even this camp shelter, which smelled of mice and accumulated grime and grease, could be prettied up and kept clean, though without running water it couldn't have a bathroom. But it was absurd to think of such things when you were a migrant who wasn't a migrant, never staying anywhere long enough to make it worth while.

The smells got on Emmy's nerves, and she rose stealthily and opened a window above her bed, easy and gentle, not to waken the now snoring family. The spicy air was gratefully cool, and Emmy drew in deep breaths of it and drifted near sleep.

Miss Kay had not yet succeeded in getting the camp owners to put in screens, though she was trying easy-like, so as not to annoy the boss. Emmy's doze was broken by the persistent whine of a mosquito round her face. The rest of the family seemed to be bothered in the same way, for Pa was thrashing from side to side, and Chad was making explosive noises in his sleep. Finally he sat up, crying, "Help, Zaskov, help! Arrows from them space ships!"

Pa said, "There, son. Easy does it. Yo're safe as a bug in a rug."

Chad lay down. He was never scared when he knew Pa was near.

Pa muttered to Ma, "Kids is sure a worry."

Ma's answer was undistinguishable.

"Sue, ain't you going to say nothing to Emmy? About that Lucero fellow?"

"He's — a good boy."

"A migrant worker? A furrin migrant worker?" Pa's tone was outraged.

"But what else — is there for her? She needs — young folks."

"You never went kiting around with no fellows when you was sixteen."

"Soon's you came along, Charlie — "

"Plenty of the Glen Lake biddies said you was too young to know what you was doing then. Sure upset your life, Susie girl."

Emmy pulled her pillow over her head. She felt that she was overhearing what was not meant for her; something absurd, besides. Pa and Ma were around forty-five. They treated each other sensibly, like mere acquaintances. The only time Emmy even heard them use first names was when they thought nobody could hear — like tonight.

7

Escape?

WHERE EMOTIONS were concerned, Ma was as reticent as Emmy. Next morning she kept her eyes away from her daughter in a way Emmy had long ago learned to read. Ma felt she must talk seriously to Emmy, and she dreaded the necessity. Indeed, in these thickening silences of hers she seemed to find it almost impossible. When the three workers went to their day's task she had not yet spoken.

All that day Emmy tried to keep her mind on the picking. Refugio and Andrés and some of the other Luceros were working another row of trees, with an aisle as broad as a highway between. Whenever she could, Emmy kept a tree between her and Andrés's seeking eyes. Even with that stout leafy shield, he often found her.

Snip — drop — snip — drop — with the pungent lemon oils strong in Emmy's nostrils and a crick in her neck and a tired ache in her arms. *Snip — drop — snip — drop* — and a gentle cascade of waxy fruit into the basket. The sun climbed till it struck at her from straight above her broad aisle, intensifying the smell of lemon and of spoiled alfalfa, used as a mulch; sharpening the tickle of dust, product of an unusually dry season.

Since it was noon, she lay flat on her back in the shade, and, after she had rested a little, pulled from her jeans pocket a crushed packet of sandwiches and munched them. Still out of sorts with Pa, she answered his remarks with monosyllables; and Chad made no remarks. Emmy hurried to get back to her picking before the Luceros should find her. She managed to avoid her friends until after supper that night.

Then Refugio called to her gaily, "How's about that double date? My boy friend says it's okay by him."

"I have to ask Ma," Emmy said, pinning up a dish towel to dry.

She went in and stood awkwardly beside the pallet where Ma lay. "Ma, is it okay if I go on a double date tonight? It's Saturday, so I can rest tomorrow."

"Double date?" Ma asked.

"Refugio has a boy friend, see, and he has a car. He'd take Refugio and Andrés and me riding. Dancing, too, maybe."

"Public dance hall? Pa would never — he's upset enough — and those cars — " Ma lifted herself on one elbow and gazed piteously at Emmy. "Emmy, kids in a car — "

"They aren't such kids, Ma." Emmy spoke impatiently. "They're all older than I am. Ma, I got to have a little fun sometimes. Seems like I just got to."

The shack, bare and grimy, with nothing beautiful, nothing even comfortable, closed on her like a trap.

"I don't mind not dancing. Not much. I'm awful clumsy at it anyway, the few times I've tried. But just the ride, Ma."

"You — sure Andrés won't think — ?" Ma asked diffidently.

Emmy grew hot. "I told Andrés. I said I didn't want to think about — about such as that. Not for years yet. Ma, it isn't because he's Spanish? Miss Marthann says it's plain wrong to despise other kinds of folks."

Ma sighed heavily. "Makes a sight of difference who you marry. If you hanker after things and he — he doesn't. Once you care for a person — so be awful careful, Emmy Lou."

Coming from Ma, as Ma had been of late, this was a long and intimate conversation, and Emmy yearned to end it. She leaned over and patted Ma, not to seem abrupt, and coaxed, "I can go, Ma? Tonight? Andrés will take good care of me." When Ma remained silent, Emmy whispered hoarsely, "Oh, Ma, just working and sleeping, and never any fun — "

"Well — but not the dancing."

Emmy dashed through the dusk to the bathhouse and

took another shower. Showers were wonderful — such an easy way to get all-over clean. Wonderful just to soap herself and scrub hard and let the warm water flow over her and wash away the suds and most of the lemon smell. Wonderful to push her hair briskly into shape with damp hands. Wonderful to let the cold water rush out and needle away the tiredness. And there were lots of people who took showers for granted.

Refugio was using the next shower stall, a bathing cap over her head to preserve her permanent. She shouted at Emmy above the noise of the water, and Emmy said "Mm-hum," and "Hm?" and followed her own thoughts. Finally, Refugio in a skimpy bathrobe and Emmy in an old coat of Pa's, they dashed back to their shacks to dress.

Emmy put on her one skirt — she had had to buy it because some schools did not allow jeans — and a sweater. She knotted a little scarf around her neck, like Miss Kay's, and tied a ribbon round her damp curls. She was joining a spic and span Refugio and an Andrés with his cherished guitar when a long low-hung roadster shot down the road between the shacks and stopped, glimmers of twilight catching on its chrome trim.

Emmy found the driver even more interesting than his car. The first sight of the fair head above the wheel turned her dizzy. But when the boy leaned on the horn and swiveled toward them, she saw that he did not in the least resemble Phil Carter.

Andrés whistled. "Gosh, sis, you sure that's his own car?"

"Want me to ask for a squint at the bill of sale?" Refugio asked pertly. "Sure it's his. He told me where he bought it. Ain't he a looker?" she added under her breath.

Emmy nodded, thinking that she hated his kind of good looks, though they made her heart beat unevenly. His blond hair had been swept back by his speed. When the light from the Lucero door struck it, Emmy thought, it gleamed like polished brass. His head was jauntily high, and his eyes seemed to be roving restlessly across the little group, around the tents and shacks nearby.

"Hi, babe!" he saluted Refugio. "Whatcha waiting for? Let's not waste any more of this fine large evening. How you like my little tin buggy? Take your breath away?"

Mrs. Lucero was slowly approaching them, as if her sparkling spirits were dimmed for once. Without looking at her, Refugio said, "Mamma, this is Jack, like I told you. Jack, meet my brother Andrés and my girl friend, Emmy. They're the ones that are going along."

"Hiyah, bud and pretty-face," said Jack, ignoring Mrs. Lucero. "All set for a big night?"

Emmy took a deep breath. "Ma says — not any dancing," she said apologetically, looking from Refugio and Andrés to Jack.

Jack flopped dramatically against the steering wheel. "No dancing!" he mimicked in a high squeak, and turned his head pointedly to survey the shacks again. "Ma's little girl too nice, is she?"

Refugio murmured impatiently to her friend, but Andrés said, "Emmy's nice, all right. Want to make anything of it?" He took a step toward the car, his shoulders lifted.

"Aw, keep your shirt on, bud." Jack threw a leg over his car door and shook back his hair. "Sure your girl's nice. Anybody can see she's nice. And if it isn't to be dancing, that's okay by me. We'll take this little old buggy on a good stretch of road and let her out. See if she can do a hundred and twenty like they say. Okay?"

Again Emmy felt as if she were two girls. One wanted to run back into the shelter and stay with Ma. The other burned with eagerness to ride in that long, low, unbelievable roadster, to go flying down the highway with the wind blowing through her hair.

"Not too awful fast, young man," Mrs. Lucero urged.

"Oh, no, not too fast, Mamma," Jack echoed her in a tone Emmy resented.

In the end, they got into the car, Andrés and Emmy in the back seat, Refugio in front with Jack. Emmy was awkward about stepping in, it was so different from climbing into the cab of a truck, or pulling herself into the box.

But it was as thrilling as she had dreamed. Drab, everyday life floated away and was lost behind her. Even the soft California air stung her cheeks to numbness. Her hair blew so wildly that the ribbon kept coming off, and finally Andrés said, "Here, kid, let me put it in my pocket or you'll lose it."

Emmy shook her head and tied the ribbon tighter, a curious feeling inside her, like a vacuum. Phil had carried her ribbon in his pocket on That Day, which now seemed to Emmy the dark turning point of her life.

They overtook a train on a track alongside the pavement. Jack took both hands from the wheel and waved them over his head. "Throw your old has-been on the next dump, brother!" he yelled, jamming his feet on the gas.

Refugio said, "Gosh, we're flying!" as they streaked past rear cars — center — locomotive.

Emmy gripped the edge of her seat. Jack was like a tight-wound toy, she thought, or like a man in a fever.

"Too fast, Jack, too fast!" Andrés shouted above the roar of their going. "Don't be a stupid fool, kid — "

"Please!" Refugio begged, clutching at him.

Gradually he brought the catapulting car to a more moderate speed. Emmy shut her eyes and sat back limply.

"It was kind of fun at that," Andrés was saying, and she opened her eyes and looked at him, shaking her head. "You're right, though," he conceded, and leaned forward to speak to Jack. "Say, kid, if that's your speed, just turn around and take us home."

Arrogantly Jack tossed back his hair. "Sissies," he

sneered. "Okay, we'll take it easy. Easy as a carful of old bags."

For a while he did maintain a reasonable rate. Again Emmy could notice that the moon was vast and mysterious and the air pungent with trees and shrubs. Their car drove a tunnel of light before it, and approaching cars often signaled angrily for Jack to lower his headlights. He paid them no heed.

But it was beautiful and wild and free, Emmy thought, and lovelier still when Andrés took up his guitar and began to sing as he plucked it. Emmy's voice trembled with happiness as she hummed. Andrés also seemed stirred, for his free arm moved across the seat back till his hand clasped Emmy's farther shoulder. She stiffened under the touch.

The quiet loveliness was rudely shattered. With a shriek of skidding tires the car turned in to a drive-in, flinging Emmy against Andrés and his guitar. Brakes squealing, it drew to a stop under the floodlights, and a pertly uniformed car hop leaned her elbows on the front car door.

"What's the big hurry?" she demanded. "And what's it going to be?"

Jack's arm also lay across his companion's shoulders, pulling her close. "Beer the best you got for us?"

Emmy caught her breath. "Not me. That's one thing Pa — "

"Not for me either, then," Andrés said. "A coke and a hamburger for Emmy and me, thanks."

"So-o?" Jack drawled. "Okay. This time. Cokes and hamburgers for all us Sunday School kiddies."

In spite of the sneer, the hamburger tasted wonderful to Emmy as they drove on. The crispness of toasted bun, the succulent bite of onion, the hot beef with its smoky barbecue tang were delicious. Again Jack broke the flow of her contentment. When he had flung out his coke bottle and his waxed paper, he dug into his pocket and brought out cigarettes, holding two back over his shoulder.

Andrés shook his head. "Got my own, thanks. And Emmy don't smoke." He leaned closer, staring at the proffered cigarettes, and his voice changed. "Take one of mine, sis. Kid, that wouldn't be — ?"

"Kid, wouldn't it, though!" Jack's voice had a flaring, taunting edge. He had lighted one of his cigarettes, and drew on it deeply while Andrés, still sitting forward, audibly sniffed at its smell. "You don't look like a sissy, bud. And you don't know what you're missing."

Andrés answered with a new mature authority. "Listen, Jack. You turn this crate around and take us home. Pronto."

Swearing under his breath as the cigarette hung from the corner of his mouth, Jack swerved the car crazily around in a U-turn, the shrieking rubber sending up a burnt stench. Furiously he spun the wheel to right the vehicle, and headed it in the direction from which they had come.

The next minutes were like a nightmare. The car screamed down the black highway strung with flashing headlights. Emmy clung to Andrés with both hands, too frightened to speak. The roaring roadster overtook and passed car after car, followed by the bleat of their indignant horns. It skinned past the abutment of a narrow bridge. It hurtled madly toward the black bulk of an underpass, and at the last instant avoided it with a screeching swerve.

Emmy's thoughts spattered out of her mind in broken bits: "If I get home alive — Father, who art in heaven — Phil will read about it — and Miss Marthann — "

A new sound pierced the roar and squeal, and rose higher and higher behind them. Andrés's head jerked round, jerked back. "Jack, you dope, the cops!"

The roadster gathered speed. It hurtled past other cars, while Emmy dropped her face against her knees. The police siren grew fainter behind them.

"Thank God, we're almost home," Andrés said.

Then came the tremendous splintering crash. Emmy felt herself held in a grip that kept her from catapulting forward. The siren screamed louder, higher.

She opened her eyes. The car had smashed into a tree by the roadside. Jack and Refugio sat crumpled and still in the front seat. Andrés put a hand over Emmy's mouth, opened to cry, and he lifted her bodily, kicking loose the jammed door.

Though not much larger than she, he staggered out of the car with her, set her on the ground well off the pavement, gave her a little push. "Run!" he commanded. "Camp's right ahead. Get home and to bed. Nobody's got to know."

He darted back to the roadster, leaving Emmy trembling alone in the dark.

8

First Payment

BEFORE EMMY could move, before she could utter a word of protest, Andrés was slipping into the back seat of the roadster. He was scarcely settled when the police car drew to a shrieking stop, its light splitting the dark.

Sick and faint with shock and fear, Emmy sank to the ground. Probably the unconscious action kept the relentless lights from finding her. She was so near that she could hear what Andrés and the officers were saying, though she was too dazed to make much sense of it.

"Didn't I see a girl in the back seat with you, kid?"

"I grabbed my guitar up against my shoulder when that crazy fool started cutting loose."

"Mmmmm." That was the officer, and his tone was dubious.

Another peremptory voice broke in. "Looks like that stolen job we've been watching for."

"What you know about this heap, young fellow?" the first officer asked sharply. "Where d'you lift it?"

"Honest, I don't know nothing," Andrés declared. "Never seen it till Jack showed up with it tonight. Mister, hadn't something ought to be done for the kids? You think they're bad?"

"You'd better be worrying over your own hide," an officer grunted.

Andrés spoke huskily. "She's my sister, and she's a good kid."

"Well, we radioed first off for the ambulance."

The other patrolman uttered an exclamation. "This may turn out to be more than car stealing. Look what the driver was smoking."

"A reefer!"

They were interrupted by clangor of siren and bells, glaring headlights again probing the underbrush where Emmy crouched. In the confusion she crept away through the dark, feeling stained and hunted. Near though the shack was, she had hardly strength to reach it.

Except for a murmur of voices, it was dark and still. "It's you!" Ma breathed out the words like a sob. "Awful crash — just now — "

"Glad you had enough sense to get in early," Pa growled.

Shaking and fumbling, Emmy undressed and got into bed.

"Whyn't you say something?" Pa asked sharply. "Sulking because yore ma wouldn't leave you dance?"

His words released Emmy's pent sobs. They shook her in long spasms, almost inaudible.

"Emmy! Emmy Lou!" Ma cried in alarm. "Nothing — nothing happened?"

Weakly Emmy wailed, "Oh, Ma! Oh, Ma, it was so awful!"

When she had gasped out the fragments that were clear to her, Pa yanked on trousers and shoes and strode from the shack. He soon returned. "They already carted off the ones that was hurt. Andrés, too, seems like."

"And Mis' Lucero?" Ma asked.

"Seems like the Luceros don't know yet."

"Got to tell them, Emmy."

"Oh, Ma."

"Reckon she's right," Pa admitted. "They'd ought to know. Funny they never got up to see what the crash was. But neither did we."

Shakily Emmy pulled on a dress, slid her feet into sneakers, and followed Pa. At the Lucero door they rapped, calling softly.

Uproar followed their story. "I didn't take to'm from the first!" moaned Mrs. Lucero. "My babies, oh, my babies! Papa, we got to get dressed and go. Are dead! Are dead, the beautiful ones!"

"Two more angels for the good God," Mr. Lucero muttered in his own tongue, the traditional phrase of submission roughened with pain.

Once she fell asleep, Emmy slept heavily. She woke to see Ma trying to start breakfast. Feeling drained and battered, Emmy pulled on her clothes and took her mother's place at the little stove.

"What did they find out?" Breathlessly she nodded toward the Lucero shack. "Is Refugio bad hurt?"

Pa nodded. "She's serious, they say. May pull through, though. The fellow's worse. Don't know nobody. Chest crushed against the steering wheel, seems like."

"And Andrés?"

"In jail. Pretty mess, the whole thing. Stolen car and maybe a tie-in with one of them marijuana rings."

Emmy fell to shuddering. "Andrés — he made sure I wouldn't get into it," she mumbled, crooking an elbow over her face.

When the Luceros appeared, Mrs. Lucero disheveled and tear-stained, and the younger children silent with awe, they could add no information. Mr. Lucero, his lean, sharp face aged overnight, got into his car and went after a newspaper.

Coming back he silently held out the sheet. The headlines said: NEAR FATAL TRAFFIC CRASH MAY LEAD TO HEADS OF DOPE RING.

"Read it off, no?" Mr. Lucero suggested, and Emmy read, the paper crackling in her tense grasp.

The story said that two young Mexicans and a youth still unidentified had been apprehended in a roadster recently stolen in Los Angeles. A quantity of reefers had been found in the glove compartment and in the driver's pockets. The only one of the car's occupants who was conscious gave his name as Andrés Lucero, a migratory farm laborer. Lucero suffered only mild bruises and abrasions.

"A — abra — ?" Mrs. Lucero inquired, wringing her hands.

"Skinned places," Emmy explained, and continued reading.

Lucero said the girl was his sister, aged eighteen, but disclaimed knowledge of the driver's surname and of the fact that the car was a stolen one. The pursuing patrolmen were at first under the impression that there was a fourth passenger, but said they had apparently been misled by a guitar young Lucero was carrying. The girl and the driver are in the hospital under guard, and Lucero is being held in jail.

"Curtains for Andy." His brother Joe spoke bitterly, spitting out the toothpick he had been using mechanically while Emmy read. "They won't take his word for nothing. He's a Mex."

"But he had no idea the car was hot," Emmy stuttered.

Joe shrugged, and Mrs. Lucero spread hopeless hands.

"And — and the reefer. When Jack offered us one, Andrés made him bring us straight home. Andrés was mad when he saw what it was Jack was smoking."

Again Joe shrugged. "Fat chance they'll believe him."

"But Jack could tell them — "

"If he comes out of this. And if it suits him to come clean. Just one thing you can count on with a guy that's hooked on marijuana — that you can't count on nothing." His glance sharpened with question. "How come you wasn't in the car, Emmy?"

"Andrés. He dragged me out and put me where the bushes were thick. At first I couldn't make out why."

Clasping her stout body with both arms, Mrs. Lucero wailed her pride and sorrow, even while she eyed Emmy somewhat resentfully. "My Andrés! Was like him to do so."

Emmy nodded soberly. "What can we do to get him out of there?" she asked practically.

"We go ask Miss Kay," his mother proposed. "Is better that an Anglo talk to Anglo police."

Soon after, Miss Kay and Mr. and Mrs. Lucero went away together, all looking hopeful. "We no say nothing about your Emmy," Mrs. Lucero told the Lanes in a grudging undertone, frowning and shaking her head. "My man say it what Andrés would wish."

When they came back, their jaunty hopefulness was quenched. All were dispirited. The Luceros dejectedly retreated to their own four walls and to an ensuing storm of questions and outcries. Miss Kay dropped limply on one of the Lanes' box seats.

"It's positively the limit," she said explosively, and then lowered her voice, glancing at the thin walls of the shelter. "Oh, I realize they have a peck of trouble with Spanish kids. Poor kids — life's so drab for them. But it's a shame to let the reckless ones blacken anyone so decent as Andrés. I told them how long I'd known him, and how he'd never been in a single serious scrape, far as I ever heard. How the Lucero family never did have a brush with the law, a big family like that. But, oh, no!" She flung out her hands in a gesture like those of her beloved Spanish. "I wasn't at the scene of the accident, so my testimony isn't worth much." She rose wearily. "Well, I suppose tomorrow's another day."

It was when tomorrow came that Emmy's troubled thoughts drove her to Miss Kay's little house, the borrowed book in her hand. She pushed past three children on the doorstep, waiting for school, which would open in an hour and a half.

"Hi!" Miss Kay greeted her, listening to the morning newscast while she breakfasted with her co-worker, Miss Amy, at the scarlet table. "You don't look as if your night's sleep had done you much good, Emmy. Read that book so quick as this? What did you think of it?"

Emmy stood looking down at the book and dumbly shaking her head. "I liked the first chapters fine. But I'm not aiming to finish it, Miss Kay, thank you all the same. Every time I read, seems like I get so restless. Books — they show what there really is for a person in this world. But — oh, Miss Kay! If I got to live like Pa and Ma — and Luceros — well, looks like I better not think about books and such."

"Oh, now, now, now!" Miss Kay hastily set down her cup of coffee and motioned Emmy to a chair. "Why on earth should you have to live that way? Thank heaven this is America. This is the twentieth century. You can build your own life."

Emmy shook her head, one small, hopeless shake. "I — I feel kind of tied — Andrés — "

Miss Kay spluttered, while Miss Amy delicately pretended to be elsewhere. "Emmy Lane, you baby! You're too young to be tied to anyone. And Andrés — But isn't this awfully sudden?"

"Yes, ma'am. But now he did this for me, seems like I have to — "

"I haven't got this quite straight. Just what did he do for you, Emmy?"

"He toted me out of the car into the bushes, where the cops wouldn't see me. He must have known it would help him and Refugio if they had me to testify, but he made out there was nobody else in the car. And made his folks promise not to tell, either."

"If that doesn't beat the Dutch," Miss Kay exploded.

"So I want to go and testify," Emmy said.

"Have you told your parents that?"

"No, not yet. But this is something I've got to do whether or no."

Miss Kay was already on her feet. "First we'll tell your folks."

"First you'll drink that coffee," Miss Amy scolded, coming back on the scene. "You can carry along a piece of toast and eat it as you go."

Pa was sullen. "One thing us Lanes been proud of: our good name. Never been in no trouble with the law, in no way, shape, form, or manner. I guess Emmy best get to work in the grove like always. She wasn't to blame. Why stick her neck out?"

Emmy said, "Luceros have never been in trouble, either."

"And that will count for the young punk," Pa argued. "He'll come out okay. Just keep mum and you'll see."

Emmy's voice was frightened but positive. "Pa, I can't. Ma, you see, don't you?"

"Reckon so, Emmy," Ma agreed, ineffectually digging at a burnt place on her frying pan and not looking at Pa.

Pa threw her an astonished and indignant glance and spatted his hands together. "Okay, then," he rumbled. Emmy knew he would have roared or bellowed if Miss Kay hadn't been there. "Okay, go and get yore name spread all over the papers, if that's the way you want it. If you and yore ma can stand it, I reckon I got to."

Emmy's heart sucked downward. Her name in papers all over the country? Miss Marthann reading about the escapade, with its dark, soiled edges? Phil? Abbie, turning up her neat nose and saying, "Well, Phil, what did I tell you?"

For an instant, Emmy hesitated. Then she said, "When do we go, Miss Kay?"

The interview was easier than Emmy had expected. She and Miss Kay sat facing the juvenile judge across a table, and Emmy could see herself in a mirror behind him. She had taken pains to comb her hair smooth and wet and tie it back primly, so as to look sober and respectable. The wetness had made it curl more vigorously than ever, and it stood up around her face in a cloud of ringlets. Emmy had begun to use a little lipstick, but today she had left it off. Her face was without color except for its deep tan and the blue eyes, even bluer in the dark circles left by shock and poor sleep.

The judge looked at the card Emmy had filled out. He wasn't austere and unapproachable as Emmy had expected. He was just a clean-shaven man who looked as if he had children of his own.

"Emmy Lou Lane, sixteen," he read, and smiled reassurance at her. "Your parents are migratory farm laborers?"

"No, sir. We're — peddlers, I guess you'd say. Baskets and rustic furniture. We just work in the crops when we get short of cash."

"And how long have you known this Lucero family?"

"Off and on since I was less than six, sir. More than ten years."

"Have you seen signs of their — taking things?"

Emmy tightened her lips and shook her head, unconsciously stroking the polished table top with her calloused fingers. "Oh, no! No, sir."

"Or having any of this marijuana? Reefers?"

"Oh, no, sir, they don't hold with such as that. Hard liquor, either. Wine, yes, and beer, but not hard liquor or dope."

"But how about this roadster?" the judge asked, leaning his elbows on the table and studying Emmy's face. "How can you be so sure young Lucero had nothing to do with stealing it?"

"Oh, because, sir! He didn't even dream it was hot.

Refugio either. She said Jack had just bought it."

After he had talked to Emmy a long time, the judge had her make a full statement, with a stenographer taking down her words, and another young woman to act as witness. She would not need to appear in any public hearing, he said.

Emmy paused in the doorway and looked back anxiously, shaking her head as if to encourage a denial. "Will my name get into the papers?" she stammered.

He laid a friendly hand on her shoulder. "I think not. Under age, and with a clean record. No, Emmy, I think we can promise not to divulge your name."

Emmy's face flooded with color. "Thank you, oh, thank you, sir!"

The judge had given them passes to see both Andrés and Refugio. As Miss Kay's little coupé carried them to the jail, Emmy found herself giddy with thankful relief. "Divulge," she kept repeating to herself ludicrously. "Next time I go to school I'll look that one up in the dictionary." Next time? According to her present plans there would be no next time. The thought made her feel empty and lost.

The glad eagerness of Andrés's greeting quickly faded. "Emmy, why'd you come here?" he asked gravely. "You ain't mixed up in this mess at all."

He looked so boyish and so forlorn that Emmy tried to speak with more warmth than she felt. "Andrés, you were just wonderful, and I'll never forget it. But of course I wanted to help. Miss Kay and I, we went to the judge and told him the whole story."

"It was the only honest thing for Emmy to do," Miss Kay answered Andrés's scowling protest. "And I feel quite sure that you and Refugio will be cleared."

Andrés flushed darkly, and a muscle in his jaw tightened and loosened, tightened and loosened, before he could speak. His dark eyes had even more than their usual luster when at last he said, "Emmy, you're sure okay. You're as swell as they come. Emmy, remember what I said to you — was it only day before yesterday?"

"But, Andrés — "

"Emmy, I'll wait till you're seventeen," he interrupted her, "even without no promises from you. Remember, Emmy."

When they reached the hospital, they found that Refugio was not yet allowed visitors, though she was off the critical list. Her worst injury had been a severe concussion, sustained when her head banged against the windshield. She had been lucky not to be thrown from the car.

Miss Kay asked about Jack. He was no better.

"Not able to throw any light on the dope ring, then?" she asked.

That was not quite the case, they told her. In his delirium he had muttered names that proved to be those of men who had sold him his marijuana. Further, his wallet had disclosed the addresses of his parents. His mother had flown from New York City and his father from San Francisco. Everything possible was being done for the boy, but hope for his recovery was slight.

Reaching camp again, Miss Kay reported to the Luceros, and then rejoined Emmy at the Lanes' shelter, inquiring after Mrs. Lane. Ma was in bed, eyes closed and color ghastly, and Pa hovered over her anxiously.

"She's took bad," he fretted. "I didn't dast go to the grove. All this business upset her awful. I sent Chad for the doctor awhile back, before Emmy come."

"I want to — get away," Ma whispered. "Pa — I can't — breathe good here."

By this time Chad was stumbling over his own feet at the door, and the doctor, tall and long-necked and overworked, followed him. He stooped to look at the sick woman, and murmured absent-minded nothings in a comforting voice. Jackknifing his long body to reach the pallet, he took her temperature and pulse, peered into her mouth, throat, eyes, with a small flashlight.

"Seems badly run down," he said. "Often happens, at her age. I should judge her blood pressure is definitely low, and she looks anemic. Those conditions are not dangerous, but they do contribute to her weakness. And to this mental condition, which I observed before. Has anyone told you that sea level isn't always the best elevation for people with low blood pressure?"

Ma's eyes pulled open. "Better where it's higher?" she asked faintly.

"Other things being equal it might be better."

He gave her vitamin and iron pills and departed. He was scarcely out of hearing before Ma fixed pleading eyes on Pa.

"Oh, Pa, the clearing at home — "

Pa's brows worked fiercely. "At home?" He stressed the word incredulously.

"The Glen." She spoke on a sobbing breath. "Pa, you can — breathe. And it's — ours."

Emmy hurried out after the doctor, and he paused in his stride. "Sir, Ma's got so strange. Not like she used to be. Reckon those pills will help? Kind of clear her thoughts?"

"She doesn't pay much attention to what goes on around her?" the doctor asked, looking at Emmy with more regard than he had shown any of them before. "Escape from reality?" he asked, as if speaking to himself.

"She's been like that a long time, not caring how things looked, even whether they were clean." Emmy flushed. "But what I wonder, sir — well, she's asking to go back to a place she always hated and despised. Acts like she wants to settle down, and Ma never had wanted that."

The doctor shook his head regretfully. "I'm sorry I can't go into this with you, young lady. Mental illness — it's out of my line. If it grows worse you had better see the psychiatric department at one of the state hospitals. These apparent hatreds of places and things, though — sometimes they aren't at all what they appear to be. But right now if you can get her physical health improved, that's about all I can suggest."

9

Change

EMMY'S NEXT FEW DAYS were unlike any that had gone before. Pa and Chad and she must finish out the week's work, needing the money it would bring, so she was busier than ever. Rising in the smoky dimness of lantern light, she got breakfast and, after it had been hurriedly eaten, straightened the place with fierce energy. She made Ma as comfortable as she could and washed a few pieces at the community laundry before hurrying to the grove, fortunately near at hand.

She and Chad and Pa always worked together, and it was Pa's pride that every crew leader was quick to see their skill and leave them without much supervision. Most pickers, except the Luceros, thought them offish, so they worked in silence, Pa and Chad never talkative, and Emmy now finding plenty to occupy her thoughts.

For poor folks, without much choice, this was a good way of life, she kept insisting to herself. The aromatic green globes of the lemon trees, which had always some blossoms along with their fruit to perfume the air, the broad avenues between them, with the tree shadows lying in one direction in the morning and shortening to nothing and then reaching out in the other direction and lengthening till by midafternoon the avenues were all shaded — didn't these make it a wonderful place to work in? The continuous calls of the mockingbirds, with their jangle of sweet dissonances, were a delight to Emmy, too, though Chad objected that they had no tune to them.

And muscles got used to the reach and the pull. If she always went to bed aching, well, Emmy had heard that even secretaries ached from their days at the typewriter.

It was beautiful — beautiful — beautiful — she reiterated definitely. She tried to find words for its loveliness. If she had to write a composition about it, for instance, how would she say it? But she wouldn't have to hunt for the right words any more, wouldn't have to write any more themes, she reminded herself. And it seemed as if hunting for the words always made things brighter and clearer to herself. And wasn't it queer how school was like a telescope, through which one looked at far trees and at stars? Stars where there had been blank emptiness?

At early dark she hurried home to get the quickest supper possible, out of cans, and to wash a few more clothes, because washing was easy here and wouldn't be when they were on the road again. By that time she was so tired that she was asleep almost before she was under her blanket. That was lucky, for days gave her too much time to think, without adding nights.

A few mornings after the doctor's visit, Emmy pulled open unwilling eyes in the lantern light and saw Pa standing before the canary's cage. He was awkwardly chirping, a thing Emmy had never heard him do, and presently he opened the wire door and reached in a big hand.

"Shore hate like pizen for yore ma to know," he muttered when Emmy sat up. "She'll feel like ever'thing's gone to pot."

He had kept his body between the cage and Ma's pallet, but it often seemed as if the only things Ma noticed were those they tried to hide from her. Now she lifted herself on one elbow so that she could see the rumpled ball of feathers on Pa's palm.

"Pa — Pet?" she asked in a thin, flat voice. At his nod, she lay down again and turned her face to the wall.

"Emmy, you put it in a little box," Pa said. "Ma, want we should take it along and bury it in the clearing at the Glen?"

Ma did not answer.

As if that were not enough, the day brought another loss. Helping pack the trunk to go, Chad lifted out the red plush box, to bed it more securely in garments they would not be needing. His eyes were fixed on his mother, as if wanting her to see how carefully he was handling her treasure.

"Watch out!" Pa warned sharply.

At the sudden admonition, Chad's arm jerked violently, and Emmy reached out to safeguard the box. Between them it fell to the floor and opened, scattering the contents. Emmy and Chad and Pa all plumped down on their knees and went fumbling after the keepsakes, glancing now and then anxiously at Ma. Everything was all right except the blue glass slipper. It had struck against the stove and broken into pieces. Ma stared dully at the fragments.

"I'll get some of the cement they use," Pa mumbled. "You know me, Ma. I can fix it most as good as new."

Ma's head shook once in weary negative, and once more she turned her face away. "No use," she said.

The other hard moments were Emmy's goodbyes to Refugio and to Andrés. They were not final, like Ma's goodbye to her canary and to her blue glass slipper, yet they lay heavy on Emmy's spirit.

Refugio was so definitely on the road to recovery that Emmy was allowed to see her the afternoon before the Lanes' departure. She smiled at Emmy, her small-boned face big-eyed on the pillow. She was basking in the attention of the other patients and of the nurses, Emmy thought.

"Gee," said Refugio, "I sure picked a wrong one, didn' I? Can you get that ride off your mind? Gee, never again! And no more Anglo dates for me, neither. 'Scuse me, Emmy. I don't hardly ever think of you being Anglo. You're so nice."

The next day Andrés was released to Miss Kay's custody. He was to hold himself ready to testify if the case came to trial. He did not go to work that day, but hung around home, giving Pa and Chad help with the loading, and keeping an eye on Emmy, who half unconsciously took care to stay close to her family.

When at last the Lanes were ready to go, Andrés held Emmy's hand tight, hopefully searching her face. His voice was husky when he spoke. "You my girl, Emmy?"

Emmy swallowed. She could not trifle lightly with the truth. "Much as I am anyone's, Andrés. I do think you're — you're swell."

At that admission his face brightened. "Hear that, Joe?" he cried. "Emmy thinks I'm swell. Whoopee. I tell you, girl, just a few years now and we'll show 'em our dust."

"Andrés," Emmy spoke breathlessly, "why don't we both get some — get some schooling? Till we're — old enough?"

Andrés stared his astonishment. "You sure got all the school you need, kid. Me, too. I can read and write and figger, can't I? We'll live the life of Riley, seeing the country while we make a living for ourself."

He didn't take me serious, what I said about stopping in one place to live. But I ought to remember, I've given up school myself. Only I can't get used to the idea yet.

She gave him a stiff little smile, though she could see he expected something more, kissed Mrs. Lucero goodbye, and got into the truck seat with Pa and Ma, while Chad dangled his legs over the tailboard. Emmy could hardly wait to get away. She felt tied, hampered, in this camp. She would write to Andrés, but until she had got adjusted to the new outlook, it would be a comfort not to have him always at hand, at once drawing and repelling her, and asking so much more than she wanted to give.

The journey to Glen Lake was interminable, even though their supply of baskets was small, and they did not stop often to peddle them. Emmy would look anxiously at Pa when they approached one of the posters that farmers and grove owners put up along the road, advertising for workers, but Pa always glanced at them automatically and then pulled his eyes away without slowing down. When Ma was feeling especially ill, they kept to a steady and moderate speed that seemed unbearably slow. Yet when Ma felt well enough so that they could go faster, Emmy did not welcome the spurts of speed.

It would be painful to reach Glen Lake. It would be hard to see Phil Carter. And how could she explain to Miss Marthann that she was no longer knocking at schoolhouse doors? That she had quit? Simply quit? Not knowing what she did, Emmy snapped her fingers to emphasize the unspoken word.

At the sound, Pa said crossly, "Cat got yore tongue, missy? When a fellow wants to think, yore tongue wags like it's hinged in the middle. When he ruther not — "

"What is there to think about?" snapped Emmy.

When Pa's anxious glance went to Ma, propped up between them for a change, Emmy roused herself remorsefully. In the light of the doctor's words, Ma's blank depression was alarming.

"Don't know why my mind's so empty," Emmy apologized. That wasn't true. Miss Kay and Andrés, Phil Carter and Abbie, Miss Marthann and Miss Mary, her first teacher, together with all the little black-haired, blue-eyed Emmys of her memory, wove in and out through her brain, leaving no room for consecutive thought.

"Hain't seen you reading, not for a coon's age," Pa said, as if rustily trying to make talk.

"Nothing to read. Every page of those Dickens books, I know what's coming on the next page. Read them so many times I got them by heart."

"Want I should pick you up a grocery magazine when we stop to buy grub? Might even stretch it to get one of them big fat ones that cost a quarter."

"No thanks, Pa. I've quit reading."

Funny, she was thinking, a few years ago they had jogged along, mile upon mile, hour after hour, with seldom any exchange of ideas. Then Emmy had pursued her own thoughts and plans, but now they pursued her. It seemed as if a person couldn't stand still, but had to move one way or the other. And Emmy, she thought desolately, was setting herself to progress backward.

That night when Pa and Chad were buying groceries, Ma roused herself to talk. As soon as she began, her eyes everywhere except on Emmy's face, Emmy knew that it was another of those times, now so infrequent, when Ma felt she ought to say something for Emmy's good.

"Emmy — "

"Yes, Ma?"

"Emmy, I — thought you'd be — glad — getting to the Glen — "

Emmy, paring potatoes, compressed her lips and said nothing.

"Can't you — can't you catch up? With that class?"

"What class?" Emmy felt stubborn.

Ma's mouth quivered uncertainly. "Phil? Abbie?"

Emmy slashed at the potato so angrily that her knife blade went through it and cut her other hand. She went on paring, and dropped the red-stained potato into the water. Finally she spoke in a strained voice. "Ma, I been thinking about it a lot, and I reckon you and Pa are right: I better stick with my own kind of folks. Phil Carter isn't my kind. As for school, it's no place for me, either."

Ma gave a little moan. "Emmy — you think Andrés — you think he's — your kind?"

Emmy's paring knife stood still. "I don't know. But he's good. And I owe him a lot."

"You — already paid," Ma whispered. "And you and Andrés — Your ideas — so different — "

At that point the truck racketed up to the tent and Emmy assumed a light manner. "Oh, I wouldn't say that, Ma. We both like to sing. And we both think I'm pretty smart." She smiled at her mother, but Ma had lapsed into the old blankness, yet not so blank as usual, for now there was anguish in her face.

When at last they reached Glen Lake, a May snow had left white patches in all the shadows, and washed the face of Mount Chautauqua till it shone rose-red against the translucent blue sky. Everything sang and sparkled.

Ma's hazy listlessness had lifted a little as they climbed to the seventy-five-hundred-foot elevation of the home clearing, though not enough so that she sat forward as Pa and Emmy did, to lift the truck up the steep grade. Interestedly the others looked around as they set up the tent, and Chad whooped at sight of the stone stove he had made during their last stop. He had noticed the barbecue fireplaces in city yards, and then had found a plan for one in the grocery magazine. Chad had been quick to see how he could follow the plan, utilizing the long-ago house chimney. And there it stood, unharmed by wind and weather.

Ma didn't go straight to bed, but pottered around, breaking off dead mullein stalks and pulling weeds in a corner of the clearing. She went so far as to pick away at the ground with a broken spade till Pa took the tool from her hands.

"Doc said you was to rest," he scolded. "Whyn't you ask Chad or Emmy to do such as this? Or me, even. If you're bent on having it done."

Ma settled back limply on her heels. "An old lilac. You said you'd fetch Pet — "

Frowning, Pa drove the spade into the hard earth around the bush, which was beaded with tiny green leaves. "I see where I got my work cut out," he grumbled. "Might as well clear the old spring up yonder and channel it down to water yore posies, long as we're stopping awhile."

Emmy cried, "Ma, isn't this a tame rosebush? The wild ones don't grow so tall around here, do they?"

Pa finally flung down the spade and stood looking at them with an enigmatic expression. "Let's put in the little box and then hyper down and get us some grub."

"Want to go along to the store, kids?" he asked, when Emmy had silently brought the box. She shook her head, refusing to meet Pa's eyes. In another minute the truck sputtered, flooded the sweet crisp air with its fumes, and dropped away downhill, leaving quiet peace behind.

When, after what seemed a long time, it returned, Chad said, "Guess who we seen, Emmy?"

Emmy shook her head.

"Abbie and her ma. La-di-da as ever."

"Hmph," said Emmy.

"And Miss Marthann."

"Yep, seen the preacher woman." Pa was lugging to the tent small sacks of sugar and flour and a packet of meat. "Says she'll be up to pass the time of day, Ma. I fetched you a magazine, Emmy," he added, dropping it on her knees. "Present for you, too, Ma."

Ma's masklike face changed slightly, though she said nothing, when Pa tossed her three packages of flower seed, one of lettuce and one each of radishes and onions.

Emmy thought, First time I ever knew Pa to plan on staying long enough for seeds to grow. Why couldn't it have been last year? Oh, why couldn't it? Now it will be hard, hard. Miss Marthann, the library, Phil Carter: in sight of them all summer, and after I've made up my mind. But, oh, land of love, what will Miss Marthann think of this rubbishy campsite?

Emmy looked around with eyes more than ever aware of the litter, the bits of sodden paper, the rusty cans left over from the last time they were there. Feverishly she ran to pick them up in a corrugated pasteboard box which she lugged over out of sight behind the tent. "Pa," she said, "didn't you use to make Ma brooms out of sticks and stuff?"

Much as Pa had glowered and growled, Emmy was thankful next morning that she had brushed up around the tent; that she had even spread a clean flour sack over the box where she set the food for breakfast, close beside Chad's fireplace. For Miss Marthann came so early that the Lanes were still drinking their coffee.

"Good! Just in time," Miss Marthann cried in her soft, light voice, holding out a big brown loaf wrapped in waxed paper that couldn't imprison its full-bodied steamy fragrance.

"A good morning to you," Pa said from the box he used for a chair. "Draw up, neighbor, and have a cup of coffee. Fetch the preacher a cup, Emmy."

Soon they were all nibbling slices of the warm bread. It was too fresh for good cutting, but marvelous for eating, its sweet crumb soaked with butter. Pa didn't hold with margarine. When the Lanes lacked money for butter, as they did oftener than not, they went without any spread, or else fried their bread or pone in drippings.

Miss Marthann lingered over a slice of bread and a cup of coffee. As Pa had said, she was easy as an old shoe. At length she glanced from the sun to her wrist watch and said, "Oh, my, if I don't get to moving, I'll never catch up with my work. What I really came for was to show you these." From her sweater pocket she pulled three letters, which she handed to Pa.

Emmy could see that they were all addressed to him, one at Fort Lupton, two at a Nevada town. All had been returned to Miss Marthann with the stamped sign, LEFT NO FORWARDING ADDRESS.

"Don't bother to read them now. I'll give you the gist." Miss Marthann leaned forward, chin on hands. "It's this new lodge they're building down in the assembly grounds. I think there would still be time to get the job if it happened to strike you."

Pa blinked up at her from his frowning regard of the letters.

"They're considering rustic furniture for the big lodge. Not exactly rustic, either, but knotty pine, quite plain. I told the foreman I had a friend who could do a first-class job. Funny how few real craftsmen you run across these days. So they asked me to write and find out if you had the summer free for them."

Pa looked at Ma, his Adam's apple working up and down above his open denim collar. Ma was sitting all of a heap, staring through an opening in the bushes, where you could see the far plains and buttes and the Black Forest, like ink spreading on a blotter.

Pa said, "Well, thank you kindly, ma'am. Any other time I'd likely say no, thank you. But the doc seems to think Ma'd ought to rest a while, and this climate might fill the bill. So I'll go see if the job's still open. Me and Chad," he added, with a half smile for the boy at his elbow.

Miss Marthann stood up, brushing the crumbs from her dress. "Another thing. Emmy, I always have a waffle breakfast for the high school seniors, and one for all the other Glen young folks that are in Obelisk High. Soon as I saw your father in the store, I thought, Well, good enough. Now Emmy can come to our breakfast!"

Emmy breathed deep and made the dive she had been dreading. "Thank you, ma'am, but I quit school. For good."

Emmy had noticed before how Miss Marthann took things in her stride, not looking shocked or angry. "Oh?" she said, glancing again at her wrist watch, brows knitted above her hazel eyes. "Walk a piece with me, won't you, Emmy? Then I won't be so late, and we can sort of discuss this."

Reluctantly, Emmy fell in step beside her, as she left the clearing.

"Now." Miss Marthann folded a smile into the firm line of her lips and looked out across the plains. "Suppose you tell me what this is all about, Emmy. Last time I saw you, you were as keen for school as any girl alive. And you're not the kind that's easy changed. What happened? If it's because your mother isn't well, wouldn't you be in a position to help her more if you went to school?"

It was like being with another girl, a close girl friend, to be with Miss Marthann. Against all her intentions, Emmy found herself pouring out the story of Andrés and the ill-fated joyride. "You see how it is," she finished. "If I'm likely to live the way Pa and Ma and the Luceros do, I'm better off without any more school. You do see that, Miss Marthann?"

"That might depend on the school. And on you. Many a time I've told Mrs. Carter, 'There's a girl who's going far.' "

Emmy smiled crookedly. "Far in a truck, like always."

"Well, anyway, you come on and eat waffles with the rest of the young folks. You haven't absolutely decided not to go to school, and I won't take no for an answer. So you put on one of your school skirts and blouses and come along. We don't dress up a lot for these parties."

With her one skirt, which was tan, Emmy wore a blue shirt that made her eyes bluer than ever in her bronzed face. When she came early into the appetizing fragrances of the parsonage, Miss Marthann greeted her with a look of relief.

"Just in time to lend us a hand, and do we need it! Mrs. Allen was taken sick in the night and I didn't get home till four, so I overslept — slept right through the alarm. Mind slipping on that apron and helping with the waffles? Two of us just aren't enough, are we, Elsie? Emmy, this is Elsie Babcock. Elsie, Emmy Lane. We borrowed two more irons, and as fast as they're baked we put the waffles in the oven to keep warm. That way we get a head start on the gang."

Dropping the bright-colored apron over her head, Emmy fell to work, quickly catching on to what was needed. She was used to adjusting to new kinds of work and new places. She was almost at ease when the rest of the girls and boys arrived, bringing with them laughter and shouts and jokes, like gifts or bouquets for the party. Wasn't she, Emmy, part of the hostessing? And she had no time to wonder what to say, or where she should put her hands and feet.

Miss Marthann had pulled the table out long, putting in all its leaves. Colored glass dishes and a flowering plant made it festive. "Well," she said, standing in the doorway to survey — and count — the gay, noisy group, "come and get it, gang. Sit down, Emmy and Elsie, you two have done your share. Abbie-gail, you got your sleep, didn't you? Mother doing all right? How'd it be if you and Pam helped serve?"

So it happened that Emmy found Phil putting in her chair for her. It was the first time since the Sunday dinner at his house, so long ago, but Emmy remembered to hitch herself up just as he pushed. "Look who's here!" he was exclaiming to the tableful, in a voice that had deepened to bass during the year. "Emmy, how you been?"

"Okay. How are you and your folks?"

The beginning was as stiff as if they had never been real friends. Emmy was relieved when everyone fell silent for the blessing, and Miss Marthann's light voice said, "Bless this food to our use, we ask Thee, our Father, and us in Thy service, Amen."

The talk burst out again, and for a while Emmy could only listen and look. It was something to have Phil there beside her, so tall and fair, even though he despised her. She felt with a twinge of pleasure that Abbie didn't think it was nice. Abbie thumped a plate with a waffle down before Emmy, and then lingered possessively behind Phil, saying that she had picked one that was extra brown the way he liked them.

The chatter grew to a torrent. "D'you pull through that humdinger of an exam, Jim?" "Have we decided to go to the Fair all together?" "You and Gail got a special seat reserved, Phil?" "Say, where you suppose we'll all be this time next year?" "In boot camp, some of us." "What d'you bet at least two of us will be riding away from the Little Log Church in a car with streamers and old shoes tied on?" "What's the big hurry? Can't you wait till we're graduated?"

Emmy made a spasmodic jab at the waffle cooling on her plate, and ate as if she were thinking of nothing else.

Phil said, "Emmy, try this butter. Mom made it. Want some honey? Or Miss Marthann's jam?"

His words were casual, but they suggested that maybe he didn't enjoy the silly talk about Abbie and himself. Besides, his tone seemed to be saying, "Can't we be at least halfway friends?"

This was not the time to tell him that she could never be his real friend again. It was not fitting for a guest to bring unhappy thoughts. That's nothing but an excuse, Emmy Lane, her self told her shrewdly. All the same, I'm going to enjoy this waffle breakfast, even if it's the last thing I ever do enjoy.

"Your mom's butter's wonderful, Phil," she said shyly. "Too good to be covered up with jam."

"Jam doesn't hide it. Just improves it," Phil retorted, ladling it on his own waffle. "Notice how much weight I've put on this year, Emmy?"

Being invited, Emmy looked at him. "You sure have, Phil."

"But you're awful thin, Emmy. Because it's the style?" He added under his breath, "The blue eyes are just the same. And the curls."

Emmy deliberately relaxed and savored her first real party. She had known a few school festivities, in classrooms, but nothing like this. Miss Marthann's living room did not resemble the modern ones in the grocery magazine, but it looked more like a room to live in, Emmy thought. Miss Marthann had an odd fancy for rag carpets, and she and the ladies had cut and sewed rags for several years, till they had enough to cover the whole floor. Some of the chairs wore cretonne covers, and the curtains were the same apricot color Emmy had noticed years ago from outside. They made the morning sunshine still brighter. The windows were full of plants, and the piano was covered with photographs of Miss Marthann's young people.

Mr. Finch, the Obelisk principal, came late, a big man with a fresh-colored face and sandy hair growing so thin that his pink scalp showed through. They all crowded together to make room for him, while Miss Marthann brought him a waffle. His blue-green eyes, rayed with laugh wrinkles, looked around the table as if he were naming over his Glen Lake students. Coming to Emmy, he stopped. "Miss Marthann! Here's something new. I'd remember this one if I'd ever set eyes on her before."

Miss Marthann said, "Oh, excuse me, Mr. Finch and Emmy. You haven't met Emmy Lane before, Mr. Finch, but I'm hoping you'll see her right along when school takes up next fall."

"Emmy!" Phil exclaimed. "Sure enough?"

She was saved from answering. One of the girls paused in her waffle to start a song, "For Finch is a jolly good fellow!" In the pleasant discord that followed, Phil could hardly have heard a reply if she had made one. The singing did not slacken. It went on to "Stand up, Mr. Finch, stand up!" and "Out the window you shall go!" and other favorites, past and present, while the principal ate faster and faster.

Finally he surrendered. He heaved himself to his feet, putting another morsel in his mouth after he was up. Solemnly he recited, "Thay, have you ever tried to thpeak a pieth or thing a thong with your mouth full of peanut butter?"

Emmy was half shocked but wholly charmed at this revelation of a big man's unbending. Imagine Pa!

After breakfast, as they milled around, clearing the table and talking, Mr. Finch beckoned Emmy to a seat beside him on the piano bench. Phil lounged after her.

"Emmy Lane, is it? And you're planning to join us next fall? She won't detract from the general pulchritude, will she, Phil?"

Even while she was enjoying Phil's chuckle of agreement, Emmy was thinking, as usual, Must learn to use them: de-tract; pulchertude. But now a definite reply seemed called for, so she spoke.

"Miss Marthann said she was hoping I could. But I'm — I'm afraid it won't be possible." Since neither boy nor man helped her, she was forced to go on and fill the uncomfortable pause. "Ma's been ailing. Still is. And, one thing and another, I had to quit school last year. Don't reckon I could catch up — "

Phil brightened. "If that's all that's eating you, forget it, Emmy. Mr. Finch, this girl's so smart she could make up a year this summer. You never saw such a smart kid."

"Look," said Mr. Finch. "Why doesn't Phil bring you over to Obelisk right now, before vacation? We'll get together the books you'll need, and have the teachers fix you up with make-up assignments. Okay?"

Once after riding for hours through a chill wet wind, the Lanes had stopped to make a fire and sip hot tea from tin cans. Emmy still remembered the life and strength and eagerness that ran through her body as the tea thawed and refreshed her. So she felt now. The tide of longing and of conscious power so flooded her that she could only sit back and twist her hands in her lap and let them talk. She didn't say yes and she didn't say no.

When the party broke up, Phil was walking at Emmy's side, saying, "Then I'll come for you Monday afternoon and take you over to Obelisk. All right? Pop doesn't go to the Springs Mondays, so I can have his car. And my last two classes are study hall, so I can come get you easy. Don't say no, Emmy."

Ahead of them Abbie was talking too animatedly to Elsie. It looked almost as if Phil had linked on to Emmy so he need not go with Abbie — and Abbie so softly pretty and proper. Under those circumstances, Emmy could not make herself stop and say, "Phil, this is all a mistake. I'm not going to school any more, ever." She made one feeble effort. She began, "Phil, I've got to — "

His response frustrated her. "Got to go to the post office? Me, too. I'll walk you down, if you've no objections."

Together they strolled down the hill to the highway, past the Joneses' grocery and filling station to the post office. The same postmistress, her round face now no higher than Emmy's shoulder, chirped at Phil like a meadowlark, and rested smiling eyes on Emmy.

"Is there any mail for Lanes?" Emmy asked, expecting none.

The postmistress swiveled to pull a sheaf of letters from a pigeonhole, and rapidly fingered through them, while Emmy teetered from toe to heel, nervously, and Phil gazed at the "Man Wanted" posters on the wall, with their sullen photographs. "Miss Emmy Lane?" She nodded, and shoved one under the wicket.

Emmy frowned at it, wondering who had written that untidy address, and where. The postmark was too dim to be legible.

Phil, his mail in his hand, turned from the criminal faces to cock an inquiring eyebrow at Emmy and the letter. "Boy friend?" he inquired stiffly.

"I don't know who it is," Emmy disclaimed, staring at the letter.

"Well, now," Phil suggested, crossing his feet in a pose of exaggerated patience, "the classic response would be, 'To avoid confusion, open before reading.' "

Giggling, Emmy slit the envelope with a bobby pin. Two sheets of tablet paper and a small photograph dropped to the floor. Both stooping to pick them up, they bumped heads sharply. When they straightened, Phil had the photograph and Emmy the letter.

"Finders keepers," Phil teased, but as he studied the photograph the fun went out of his face.

Emmy looked, too, frowning with surprise. The kind taken and finished while the subject waits, it was cheap and small. Yet even its poor quality could not hide the charm of the dark face smiling out of it, the glossiness of the waving hair, the limpid blackness of the eyes.

"Why, it's Andrés Lucero!" Emmy exclaimed.

"Too good-looking," Phil declared critically.

"But he's no mamma's boy," Emmy defended Andrés. At once she regretted the choice of that particular word.

Phil's face was flushed as he handed back the picture. "Well, everyone to his taste," he said, "as the old woman said when she kissed her cow."

Without another look at letter and picture, Emmy stuck them back in the envelope, though Phil said, "Oh, read it. Never mind me."

Emmy shook her head. Without reading it, though, she thought about it as they trudged back up the hill. What did Andrés have to say? Had there been any new developments in the case against Jack? Seeing her somber and absent-minded, Phil also became mute.

"See you Monday morning," he said shortly, and was striding away from the clearing before she could reply.

Taking out the letter, Emmy hoped miserably that Phil hadn't got a good look at the pages, all blots and misspellings.

Deer Emmy, it ran, *Did you get there O.K. We miss you bad. I gess you kno who misses you wurst. Sis is home O.K. You will be sorry to kno that Jack is paralize. For good, the doc says. Except for Jack, we are out of the mess O.K.*

Emmy, I been working like a naler. I can by a jeep before long. In time for you kno who.

Well, I guess I about wore you out with this. Remember and dont get stuck on some other fella.

Con amour,

Andrés Jose y Maria Ortega y Lucero.

All the fun of the morning drained away from Emmy. She ought not to have said she'd go to Obelisk after those books and assignments.

But since she'd promised, she could study through the summer and let that end the matter. Though the more she knew, the harder it was going to be if she married a — a letter like this one.

10

Books and Rabbits

PA AND CHAD came home from the assembly grounds with furniture plans in hands and heads. They would figure how much lumber was needed, and go over to Castle Rock that afternoon to pick out the cleanest and soundest. Luckily the carpenters on the grounds had offered Pa the use of the tools he lacked, as well as a shelter where they could store things and work. Preacher woman had likely managed that, he said.

In the full tide of talk and handwashing, Pa stopped to squint at the corner of the mirror. "Where did this freak come from?"

Emmy put on a gay assurance. "It came in a letter from Andrés today. Pa, he says we're all clear of the mess except poor Jack."

"Poor Jack?" Pa's emphasis was indignant.

"He's paralyzed, Pa."

Pa frowned at the picture. "You been to the preacher woman's?" he asked with apparent irrelevance.

Emmy turned to the waffle party with relief, even though she was uncertain of Pa's reaction to her new plan.

Pa heard, and speared a piece of bread as they sat around their box table, frowning at the fluffy slice because he didn't approve of a steady diet of store bread. His comment was surprising. "Too bad there ain't school in summer." More normally, he added, "Don't fool yoreself, though. Come fall we're taking out for Californy."

"I'm not fooling myself," Emmy snapped. "I don't plan to go to school anymore. It just seems good sense to learn a little bit more when the chance is handed to me."

Again Pa surprised her. "You really don't plan to go to school no more? Not anywheres? What's come over you?"

Emmy evaded the question. "Phil offered to take me to Obelisk Monday. In his father's car."

Pa blinked reflectively.

The trip to Obelisk was uncomfortable. Phil sat rigid behind the steering wheel and gazed ahead as if in a brown study, and, after a few polite attempts at conversation, Emmy fell silent, too. Not until they drove into the school grounds and parked amid other cars and big yellow school buses did the ice around them crack.

Emmy could not restrain a cry of delight at the outlook from the consolidated school. The village had a less gently pictorial setting than Glen Lake, but it had a breadth of view and splendor of its own. Emmy threw back her head and let the wind blow her hair. "With the sky so big and blue — and the hills quiet all around — and out yonder so wild and free — "

"You love it, Emmy," Phil said, his eyes curious.

"Oh, seems like you could let the wind pick you up and carry you on forever and ever," she said breathlessly.

As if animate, the veering wind swooped down on girl and boy and sent them scudding to the shelter of the big building.

From his office Mr. Finch spied them. "A fine, wide good morning to you, Emmy Lane! Phil Carter!" he called, looking like an elderly outsize cherub, with the sun turning his sandy frill of hair into a halo.

Emmy loved even the bleakness of the big schoolhouse, as well as its good smell of chalk dust. She murmured breathless comments to Phil, her eyes lingering fondly on rooms they passed without entering: "They learn to typewrite, too," "And there's cooking classes, and sewing!" "Aaah! a library!" Once as they passed a room where a teacher was addressing a class, a boy flung out his arms and writhed in a wholehearted spasm of yawning. "Oh," Emmy breathed in soft protest, "kids don't know what they've got."

"Look at our new-style desks in study hall," Phil bade her, his brows puckering with that same look of puzzlement and curiosity.

The teachers were responsive. One was small and sharply erect, with eyes like robins' eggs and hair like curly wheat. A dark one who stood and talked like a boy had just got her Ph.D., Phil said. One had a crew haircut and no necktie, and his voice came thundering out of his rugged face. Another of the men was small and spare and precise like a bird. They all looked at Emmy as if she were a regular person, and they all marked out what she was to study in the books the principal had handed her and Phil.

The little blue-eyed one gave her also a copy of the questionnaire her classes had been sending out to possible places of employment in the vicinity, to hospitals, hotels, restaurants, stores, factories, so that they might learn about requirements.

"Schools have such big hearts," Emmy blurted out. "Seems like they want to help a person with everything."

Phil peered at the list of employment places. "Even got our rabbit-wool industry in the Glen," he said proudly.

"Emmy," he said, when they came out and climbed into the car, "you can't mean you won't anyway finish high school?"

"Sure I mean it. I've quit."

"Is it your folks? Is your dad so dead set against it? Or is it because you're so worried about your mother?"

"They aren't set against it anymore. Not as long as I don't try to keep them stuck in one place. No, the funny thing is they act kind of disappointed about my quitting."

Frowning, Phil concentrated on driving up a sharp incline and down onto the highway. "Emmy," he burst out, "I sure don't get it. You're as crazy about school as ever, I declare you are. I never knew anybody so daft about it. You look at that big old dump as if you could eat it with cream and sugar. And you think all teachers are wonderful, even the crabs. Then why on earth? Emmy, it isn't that guy in the picture? It just can't be."

Emmy gulped. "Why can't it?"

"For one thing, you're not quite seventeen."

"I'm not engaged to him or to anybody else, and I wouldn't be for years yet," Emmy said coldly.

Phil's voice was husky. "But, Emmy, him!"

"Andrés is decent, and he's kind. What more can a girl like me expect?"

Phil left that question unanswered. "Emmy, the writing.

It looked almost — illiterate. You wouldn't be happy. You've got such an active mind."

Il-literate: ought to mean unlettered, but words are tricky, she thought. Aloud she said, "I haven't promised anything to anyone."

"That's something." Phil's tone was unsatisfied.

Should she tell him about the miserable joyride? She couldn't bring herself to the revelation, and the four miles to Glen Lake passed in a silence so stiff that it reminded Emmy of cold nights when her legs ached from being drawn up for warmth. Now it was her neck muscles and her spirit that ached.

Yet when Phil let her out at the edge of the clearing, she was unprepared for the finality of his goodbye. "No, don't bother to come in," she said, as if forced to say it against her will. "I can easily carry the books. And thank you a lot."

"No trouble. Well, I'll be seeing you. Maybe."

Emmy lifted startled eyes to his face.

"I got a job," he answered her unspoken question.

"Oh?"

"On a cattle ranch this side of the Springs. Beyond the site of the new Air Academy. Ranching's what I want to do eventually. Cattle."

"You quitting school, too?" she asked blankly.

"Gosh, no, just working summers. I'll go to Aggies when I'm through high. Want to learn all there is to know about ranching."

"Funny," Emmy said. "I'm getting a job, too. In the rabbit place. Well, so long." She choked on the word and had to turn around quick, not to let him see her face.

Summer was marching on. The yuccas bloomed and replaced their flowers with fat green seed pods. Choke-cherry blossoms drenched the air with fragrance and went their way. Lilacs came into bloom, among them the old bush in the clearing, where Ma's canary was buried. Ma pottered around, tending the rows of tiny lettuce leaves and the spearlike onion plants and the radishes. The flowers weren't up yet, for she had remembered that flowers must be planted late, up this high, else the last spring frosts nipped them.

Pa tried to joke her about her garden. "You keep it so clean you hardly leave enough dirt for things to grow in."

He and Chad worked on the furniture, at the assembly grounds a half mile away, and in between-times they went fishing. The fishing was poor, but they were both so clever about it that they usually brought back enough small trout for a meal.

Immediately after her trip to Obelisk with Phil, Emmy had turned her attention to the rabbit mill. She scrubbed herself in the stinging cold spring water, combed back her hair and tied it, put on the skirt and blouse she had worn to the waffle party. Then she took the ten-minute walk down the hill, a walk full of wild flowers and bird songs, and along the highway to the rabbit mill. It wasn't the brisk walk that made her breathless, but the fear of being turned down, after she had spoken to Phil with such assurance. She squared her shoulders and went in. There's no place to knock, she told herself, but I sure can ask, and I hope I receive, the way it says.

The man in the office asked for references, and Emmy hesitatingly gave Miss Marthann's name. Without having to look it up, he dialed a number on the desk phone, and Emmy could hear Miss Marthann's voice, faint but unmistakable.

"Jim Bates speaking." While he talked, the man unconsciously scrutinized Emmy, and his free hand folded a sheet of notepaper into a tight wad. "Fine, thank you. And you? Young lady just gave you as a reference. Wants a job here. Name Emmy Lou Lane. Okay, okay. Yes, we sure will take care of her right, Miss Marty, and thanks a lot. 'Bye now." Smiling at Emmy, he cradled the telephone. "Sorting wool suit you? Okay. Let's get started."

Soon Emmy had a mask over nose and mouth, for protection from floating fibers fine as spiderweb, and was working with a group of the village women and girls.

"Don't you go pushing off that mask," Elsie Babcock warned her. "The fuzz can do a lot of harm. Of course it's extra bad for me," she added with a degree of pride, "because of my throat. Get laryngitis two-three times every winter, and, boy, when I get it I can't speak above a whisper for a week."

Emmy had much to report when she went home for

dinner that noon, not having brought a lunch. "They're all right. The ladies do kind of gossip about folks, but nothing bad. And the girls talk about clothes and dates and such as that. Elsie is the one I know best. I met her at that waffle breakfast. She's working to earn more clothes," Emmy added with a sigh.

"Well, I reckon you can use some of your wages that-away, too," Pa granted grudgingly. "I can see we wouldn't have no peace if you didn't. But what do you mean, sorting? I don't get the straight of it."

Emmy explained how the silky soft stuff was sold by length, with the longest fibers worth the most. Emmy had seen a little of the spinning and weaving, and had learned that they presented problems, since the wool was so fine as to generate electricity that caused trouble in ordinary machines. For a while girls spun it on old-fashioned wooden spinning wheels, but now the technicians had overcome mechanical difficulties to a great degree. "The knitting wool and the cloth and the blankets—they're as delicate as those furry pasqueflowers," Emmy finished wonderingly.

"Looks like you learnt more than you worked." Pa's tone might be critical, or it might be secretly proud.

"Elsie told me some, while we were sorting. But they like for us to know. They said when there was time I could go see the rabbits, up the hill from the factory. Elsie says they're like big white puffs of milkweed."

"Rabbits are?" Chad protested.

"Yes, sir. And there's just as much to rabbits as there is to cattle," Emmy declared rashly. "Besides, you don't have to kill them to make your money, like you do with cattle and foxes and mink. The only thing I don't like about it is being cooped up indoors and having your nose and mouth bandaged."

It would be gratifying to tell Phil what she was learning about the rabbit industry. If ever she had the chance.

Miss Marthann came up at once to see how Emmy liked the new job. She came walking fast, because she never had time to stroll. She would have asked Emmy to help her with vacation school, she said, if Emmy hadn't been working. This was only the second year, she added with a sigh, that Phil hadn't been her right-hand man.

"Doesn't Abbie come over and help?" Emmy had to ask it.

"Oh, yes, Abbie comes over," Miss Marthann said without enthusiasm, and then added, as if there were a connection, "Emmy, what about this boy that writes to you from the Coast? The one you told me a little about? Not that I want to intrude."

"Andrés? I'll show you his picture, but — " Emmy left the sentence dangling and went into the tent to get the picture from the mirror, where she kept it to remind herself.

Eyes narrowed, Miss Marthann studied the cheap little print. "He's — good-looking," she said, nodding her head vigorously. "I can see how any girl would find him attractive. And he looks as if he might be — good, too. But, Emmy, does he care about the things you care about?"

Almost what Ma had said. "How do you mean?" Emmy asked evasively.

"Books. Schooling. Amounting to something."

"Well, like I told you, Andrés is clean and decent and kind. And that isn't so common."

Again Emmy noticed that it wasn't so much what Miss Marthann said as what she didn't say, and the way her brows drew together over her light, bright eyes, and her mouth firmed in a rueful smile, as if something hurt. "Well, to change the subject, Emmy," she said briskly, "I may as well admit I hoped you'd take Phil's mind off Abbie. Abbie-gail."

When Emmy only stared, too startled to speak, Miss Marthann hurried on, half laughing. "Oh, don't misunderstand me. That little girl's so pretty you can't blame a boy — and in her way she's smart. Competent. My goodness, I can remember when she was knee-high to a duck, and even the way she'd blow her little nose was competent. She'll make a fine wife for someone." Miss Marthann widened her eyes as if wondering for whom. "But not for Phil."

Even though she could not think which way to look, Emmy wished Miss Marthann would go on. Miss Marthann evidently thought she had said too much already. In her characteristic way, she consulted the sun and then her watch, and gave a swift exclamation. "Left a cake in the oven. What do you know! Devil's food, too, with lots of eggs. One of the ranch women brought me two dozen and I thought I'd be extravagant for once."

11

Pain and Pleasure

SUMMER NO LONGER marched slowly along its benign and blossomy road. It picked up speed like a train running downhill, clackety-clack, faster and faster. Wild roses bloomed and faded, spiraea, pentstemon, gilia. Grosbeaks sang their lovely song and catbirds copied them. Hummingbirds zoomed overhead like midget airplanes. The bird songs mounted to a crescendo and grew still. Aster and goldenrod took the place of the early flowers.

One evening after supper as the Lanes sat before the tent, around the folding table Chad had devised, Emmy sighed deeply. "What you reckon, Pa? Ma? Last night I finished my last assignment. I could start even with the rest, if I was a mind to."

"You done real good," Pa grudged. "It's kind of pushed you, too, I seen that, with yore job and looking after things here. Though, like I said, you've made yoreself extra work by being so fussy," he hastened to add. "A little dirt never hurt nobody. But it's lucky you're done. Noticed how the robins are ganging up to take off? And last night I heard wild geese honking. If you kids can keep your eyes open long enough tonight, you'll see birds against the full moon. Us Lanes got to spread our wings, too."

Yes, Emmy had noticed. The noisier chatter of the robins had hurt her ears. The lisping autumn call of the chickadees had lost its sweetness for her.

Chad said, "Few more days and Pa and me can finish off the last of them big old chairs for their parlor."

Ma drew her old sweater close. "My pa used to say, 'Listen to the crickets. Sound different. Got to go up canyon — haul down the winter wood.' "

"Sure lucky we don't have to stay where the winters is cold," Pa said, eying Ma with some surprise, because for a long time she had been talking so little.

"Crazy foreman tries to coax Pa." Resentment contended with pride in Chad's voice. "Wants we should do eating tables and benches. And those benches to put satchels on in the bedrooms. Take all fall, what he's got figured out."

A faint excitement lent momentary life to Ma's voice. "You've done — real well. Pa, sometimes autumn is pretty here — "

Pa grunted. "Them pretty autumns! Blizzards whizzing out of a clear sky. Water freezing in the radiator." He made the z's hiss like a nest of rattlesnakes.

"But then — it's Indian summer again — "

Pa was scowling his indignant amazement. "Hain't

never heard that kind of talk out of you before, Ma. You wouldn't want to winter here? In a tent?"

"Just fall, Pa — "

"You and Chad could put boards halfway up the tent walls to break the wind," Emmy suggested. "Like the doctor said, this high country does seem to perk Ma up some."

Pa shot an uneasy glance at Ma under his bristly brows. With all his rough ways, he does set store by Ma, Emmy thought, and if she thinks she'd best stay a while longer — Voicing no protest, he pulled himself to his feet, shivering noticeably, and said, "Guess I'll turn in."

Next day he did not refer to the subject. It was as if he felt that anything he said might lock a door of escape, now only lightly closed. Chad went around glowering. Ma picked the chokecherries that ripened here later than down around the village. Never before had Emmy seen her preserve fruit, but this year she made a little jelly and put it into glasses Emmy salvaged from a dump up the canyon, an unsightly heap of tins and glass amid the autumn-bright undergrowth and below the majesty of the mountains. As bad as if it had been piled in Miss Marthann's parlor. Ma stored her jelly in a cupboard Chad had made her by nailing shelves into an orange crate.

Emmy's decision to go to Obelisk came unannounced, as Ma's jelly-making had done. Just before Labor Day, she was returning from the rabbit mill in the long shadows of afternoon when a blond young woman in ankle socks and crisp housedress genially greeted her. Emmy and Chad had got acquainted with many of the Glen Lakers, and this was one they saw often. It was Lil Tudor, driver of the school bus.

"Going to be one of my passengers Wednesday?" Lil called. "Sure glad. Like to look at those black curls."

"It's a mighty nice school." Instinctively Emmy liked the driver, and she knew that Lil had a proprietary pride in Obelisk. "But we're going on to warmer country, so — "

Lil was smiling at her, but had evidently stopped listening after the first sentence. "Surest thing you know!" she cried, setting the motor of her jalopy into roaring action. Lil was always on the move, as if never able to keep up with her crowded days. "We wait the bus just five minutes overtime. Be seeing you!"

Looks like I'm being hornswoggled into going to school, as Pa would say, Emmy thought, and laughed at the ridiculous idea: she, Emmy Lane, having to be forced to go to school. But her laughter faded. It hadn't been funny to see all of a sudden that her heart's deepest desire was not best for her. Didn't her father and mother prove it? Which was the happier? Pa, without question. Which had had the more schooling? Ma, equally without question. Schooling and all that went with it had unfitted her for the roving life.

Still, she went on thinking as she walked homeward, Ma had used this unaccustomed interval for gardening and jelly-making. Perhaps Emmy ought to use it to accept what those Obelisk teachers were so willing to give her. It was not as if she couldn't earn a little at the rabbit mill after school hours and on Saturdays. And with Miss Marthann and Mr. Finch and the teachers all so kind, it seemed ungrateful not to take advantage of the opportunity. It might not be for more than a week or two.

All this she explained to the family while they ate supper.

Pa said, "Why not? So long as you keep it in mind that we're moving on soon as snow flies."

Ma nodded, her face expressionless.

Chad held his cup of tea in both hands and gazed over it in alarm. "I ain't a-going just because she does."

"Oh, yes you are, young man," Pa declared, as if he had had it in mind all along. "I ain't a-going to have no son of mine drop behind his sister. It ain't fitten. And it ain't as if you was a migrant, and the schools not willing to take you. More'n that, number work will help you with this job of carpentering. Yes, sir, as long as we're where it's handy, you can hyper along to school same as Emmy."

Passionately Chad dashed his tin cup to the ground. "You didn't go to school, Pa. Like you always says, what good does books do a fellow? I just as lief never see inside another one."

His father gulped down the food in his mouth and roared, "I'd be ashamed, if I was you, not to keep up with a girl. When you come right down to it, maybe we'd ought to take that foreman up on his offer. You could get in some good licks at this school; and if you'd help me after school, we'd ought to get the job polished off before Thanksgiving. The ready cash sure would look good, now yore ma's not able to help with the earning."

These arguments for and against were making Emmy dizzy. "But, Pa," she said faintly, "I've told folks I've quit school."

"You kids going to chew the rag all day? I'd sure like a little peace, so I could get the good of my vittles."

"But I told everyone — "

"Well, missy, that's yore lookout. You can tell 'em yore old man said differnt. Clean waste, not to get what you can when it's handy: fish or book learning, which-ever." He held out his tin plate and Emmy silently heaped it with stew. "Reckon I'll be going to Castle Rock tomorrow, to pick me out some more good clear pine. You kids can go along and get you new jeans and shirts and such as that. Crazy notion, great girls going to school in overhalls, but it's sure easy on the pocketbook."

So on Wednesday, as Lil had foretold, the two were at the bus stop, smelling richly of new cotton.

"Hi, there!" Lil greeted them as they swarmed into her bus. "Top of the morning, it's a bright and shiny day! All rarin' to go?" Without waiting for reply, she cried heartily, "Surest thing you know!" and craned her neck to count passengers.

Lil was a favorite, and most of the students relished her breezy radio quotations and her hearty phrases. Emmy noticed how gleefully they repeated these sayings under cover of the noise, as the bus charged down the highway.

"Hi, Elsie! You going to the moon today?"

"Surest thing you know! Going to the moon to take lessons in jujitsu."

Again it was, "Hi, Phil! You feeling fine today?"

"Surest thing you know. Got a headache and hydrophobia and a game leg."

At first Emmy's loyalty to big, kind Lil made her resent the nonsense, but she soon saw it was a friendly game. In the school vocabulary, "Surest thing you know!" had become a resounding "No!" and they loved Lil all the more for giving them the phrase. Except perhaps Abbie.

"Hi, Abbie!" Jim Bennett said. "You giving up your claims to Obelisk's most eligible bachelor?"

Abbie lifted her head in the gesture that best showed off the soft curves of her chin and throat. "Corny!" she retorted.

She and Phil were sitting together, and Emmy kept her eyes away from them. She tried ridiculing herself. Surely she, Emmy, didn't suppose she had any claim on Phil! Well, then, what did it matter if another girl appropriated him? Besides, Phil had not been a part of any of the other schools where she'd been as happy as a queen. Well, then, didn't that prove that he didn't matter two straws to her?

In those early autumn weeks she found Obelisk High the richest experience of all. She stopped reminding herself that this happiness would make it still harder for her to live the wandering life.

"I've never had it so good," she told Pa and Ma, though Ma seldom seemed to be listening to anything they said. Emmy knew better than to explain what made some of the difference: her father's working as a regular carpenter and cabinetmaker; her own place as part of the community, dressing just the same as all the town girls.

"Wouldn't have called it any soft snap, plugging away like you do. Though, like I said, you got nobody but yoreself to thank for a heap of yore scrubbing. Ma and I don't have to have it so fancy. I had my full of pizen-neat housekeeping before I was growed."

"Fancy! Neat!" Emmy scoffed, looking around her.

Yet even this approach to ordered cleanliness had cost her hard work. Out of her earnings she had bought sheet blankets for their pallets, and now new tin cups and plates for their meals. With Miss Marthann popping in most any time — and if Phil should come —

But Phil did not.

Yes, it was more than a full day's work to wash the clothes for the four of them, keep the place tidied up, cook most of the meals, go to school, and work at the rabbit mill on Saturdays. She had given up the idea of putting in any time there on weekdays. Studying was almost pushed out of those full days.

Since she never had a chance to study till after the

family was abed, she had rigged up a lantern out behind the tent, over her orange-crate desk. Several times she had fallen asleep while studying, and had wakened shivering,

to find the lantern chimney smoked black, another job to chuck into the next day's full program.

Yet those nights, and one in particular, were something

to remember: the mountains black around her, the sky blue-black, the stars sharp white, the Milky Way glistening like frost. The Big Dipper was out of sight behind Sundance Mountain, and that meant it was somewhere around midnight. The North Star was above her, and she could find Cassiopeia. She had learned the names of a few constellations in General Science, and somehow the knowledge had made her feel more at home in the universe. If she could know them all!

That one special night it was as still as if the world held nothing but Emmy; as if it belonged to her alone. All the village houses she could see were dark, and even the taverns over on the highway. Crickets fiddled slowly in the chill air, and somewhere an owl hooted.

A loud snuffling on the dim hillside made her blow out the lantern and creep into the tent. That would be a bear coming down to smell out any tasty garbage. Chad would have wanted to try Pa's rifle on it, but that was against the law.

Even Chad's rebellion over the long pause at Glen Lake had weakened, though not his dislike for books. Mr. Finch was serving as coach that year, and he had encouraged Chad to go out for sixth-grade football.

Pa had looked at his son with mingled pride and deprecation when Chad told him about the football. "Little squirt like you? Thought they was all big hunks of boys with broad shoulders."

Chad poked with his toe at the ground and squirmed.

"The sixth-grade fellows is mostly three-four years younger'n me," he growled. "Besides, he says I'm fast as greased lightning and tough as a pine knot."

Pa tried not to beam. "Wisht you was a little faster on the numbers. You ain't going to school just to play games, bub."

Emmy thought that these stormy mutterings of Pa's were like the thunderheads that rolled up out of the blue sky over Mount Hermon, this dry season, full of threats that were never fulfilled. When Chad came panting home late for supper on football-practice nights, Pa's roars were mild. "Fat lot of help I'm getting out of you, young man. I suppose it's no skin off yore nose if I got to go it alone and not get done before Christmas."

He was busy. They were all continuously busy, except Ma. On the dump Pa had found her an old rocking chair which he repaired stoutly. Here Ma sat in the sun and rocked when she wasn't pottering in the garden. Emmy had never seen such lettuce as Ma's, great bouquets of green and russet frills. The radishes were crisp and the onions full of flavor. The rosebush offered them a new assortment of small sweet blooms each month, and though the nasturtiums and marigolds did not flourish, they blossomed sparsely till frost. To the west of the clearing, the plants Miss Selby had identified as angelica grew five and six feet tall, lacy green with umbrellas of lacy white, and the mulleins shot up their stalks of thick-set yellow flowers.

"Angelica, do you say?" Pa ejaculated when Emmy filled a milk bottle with its foliage. "Well, I'm a ring-tailed monkey if that ain't hemlock, and pizen as it can be. Just don't you go sucking the flowers for their honey."

Pa had found another treasure on the dump: a monkey stove, he called it, small and round, with one of its spraddled legs missing. He fixed up the stove for the tent, making it more comfortable nights and mornings. Another thing that added to Emmy's comfort and Chad's was the warm sweaters they bought out of their earnings. Chad grumbled at the extravagance, but he strutted when he wore his, bright red and brand-new.

Brother and sister could even afford to buy hot meals at noon, for the government's school lunch program kept the price low. At first Emmy lunched in silence, her eyes busy. She found that some ate politely, and some no better than the Lanes. She tried not to notice Phil and Abbie, because when she looked at them she had a left-out feeling reminiscent of her days of crumpled dresses, canvas sneakers, uncombed hair. When that feeling grew painful as an aching tooth that could not be ignored, Emmy set herself to getting over it. It was up to her not to care, she told herself firmly, on a night when she lay long awake, listening to her family's slumber. She was sure this wasn't the sort of thing that was meant by the promise about asking and receiving. Anyway, she would be ashamed to bother God with anything which was so out of the question. But although she knew perfectly well that a boy like Phil Carter could never think — that way — about a girl like Emmy Lane, she did find it hard to have him despise her, or to have that Abbie act as if she owned him.

After many repetitions, her nighttime resolution helped. Emmy found that she could often avoid feeling, in much the way she could avoid smelling. And while no one could take the place of Phil, it was a help to have Jim Bennett and Angelo Baca interested in her. Emmy copied other girls in their way of responding to such attentions. She copied their slang, and their hearty way of saying "Surest thing you know!" as a negative.

More and more she fitted into the school life, so that she found herself deep in some of the extracurricular activities also, without intending to be. For the most part these were minor affairs, for she knew she must refuse important ones. The drama teacher asked her to take a part in a school play, but Emmy explained that they might have to go to California any day. She added vaguely that her father had had word that he'd have to come soon if he wanted a job in Conchita.

School plays fascinated Emmy, they were so much more touchable than movies. Besides, they had the aroma of chalk dust and books and sweeping-sawdust that intoxicated her. Since some of the rehearsals fell in her free period, she let herself be drawn into the absorbing task of prompter.

"Goodness," complained Abbie, who had a small part,

"why does Emmy Lane have to make such faces? She scares me out of a year's growth."

Even Phil laughed, and Emmy grew hot with confusion, aware for the first time that she had been trying to help the actors with expressions as well as words.

"Too bad some of the rest of you haven't Emmy's facial mobility. Such deadpans," the coach said pointedly. "It's a pity Emmy hasn't time to take a part herself. She's a born actress, and I can't say as much of most of you."

Mobility. Must use that word, one side of Emmy's mind was saying, even while the rest of her went warm with the praise.

And then, two days before the Saturday of the play, Elsie Babcock developed a case of her famous laryngitis and could not speak above a whisper. And Elsie had one of the solid supporting parts.

"Maybe it will clear up in time," the coach answered Elsie's painful whisper in consternation.

"Surest thing you know!" boomed Phil's deepening voice. "I mean, there's not a chance in a carload, coach. We've known Elsie's laryngitis since it was a baby, and once it gets hold it hangs on."

"And no one could learn the part in time."

Emmy raised a hand that looked to her as large and red as a danger flag. "I memorize easily," she apologized. "Doesn't it go like this: 'If you'd only look where you're going, or anyway — ' " While coach and players stared, Emmy reeled off the dozen speeches with only a few mistakes. She finished in a startled silence that lasted until she began to feel sick. Had she made a fool of herself?

The hush was broken by the coach, who rolled up her eyes and clasped her hands, saying, "Saved by the bell! Emmy Lane, I've a notion to keep you under lock and key till the play's over."

Emmy thought that even Pa and Ma might realize that this was something special. Ma did say, "Well — Emmy!" and her eyes filled with tears. Encouraged by this reaction, Emmy watched eagerly when Pa came home, Chad thumping along beside him. Pa was disappointing. He scowled so blackly that Emmy did not dare mention the subject until he had been softened by eating some of his supper.

Then she cleared her throat and asked, "Pa, did Chad tell you? About the school play?"

Pa snorted so that tea sprayed out over his denim shirt. "Emmy, I sure warned you what to expect. Soon as we get the job done, I says, we pull up stakes. Well, tomorrow sees it done, and us on our way."

Emmy gazed unbelieving, shaking a mute head.

"Don't go looking at me like I was some monster. I ain't doing this to spite you. You know good and well we're already late for the job we want at Conchita. We got to step on it, no two ways about that."

"But, Pa — " Emmy looked to her brother for help, but without hope. He was sitting on the edge of his box chair, hands in pockets, feet stretched toward the fire, and he refused to meet her glance. Then, to Emmy's astonishment, he burst into speech.

"Pa, at school they act like — like it mattered a heap. Even Finch does. They act like Emmy was the only one — "

Pa devoted himself in frowning silence to his food. When he refused to speak further, a ghost of Emmy's old rage boiled up inside her.

She controlled it enough to say tremulously, "Pa, they're counting on me. They've sold two hundred tickets. I passed my word."

Pa surprised her more than Chad had done. "Whyn't you say so in the first place?" he complained, almost as if he were grasping her last sentence as a way of escape. "A Lane's word is as good as his bond. That's one place I never had no quarrel with Paw and Maw: whatever they said, they stuck to, whether it was a pair of new boots or a licking. Specially the licking." Pa's brows drew down with a humorous pain. "After this you best not give yore word so easy. But I don't reckon a day or two will lose us the job, if it ain't already lost — I hope."

Until that moment Emmy hadn't fully known what the part in the play meant to her. Limply she sat back, unable to see anything beyond the happiness of the next three days. She ate without knowing what was on her plate or in her mouth. Suddenly she looked from her father to her mother and asked, "Wouldn't you both come and see it, the play?"

Ma shrank back, clutching her sweater close in the well-known gesture and shaking her head. Pa said, "Another time."

As if there could ever be another time. Yet even that thought could not dispel the rosy mists.

During the next days Emmy used every spare minute in repeating her speeches: "If you'd only look where you're going, or anyway look where I'm going — " "Absolutely not, my good man. The fat may be in the fire — " and the rest. Her short nails bit into her palms as she rehearsed the lines.

On the great evening, Emmy was on-stage when the curtain rose, and the audience shimmered before her like the highway when she was carsick, and not a word came to her mind. Luckily, Jim Bennett was the first speaker, and by the time he had finished blustering at her, in a high, unconvincing voice, her eyes had cleared, the stage had stopped swinging, and her mind had grasped her opening words: "If you'd only look where you're going — "

She was off. Everything was all right. It was more than all right, it was wonderful. She was part of this gay make-believe, and the packed audience of grownups, adolescents, and children followed her with approving intentness wherever she stood and whatever she said.

After the final curtain, Emmy was almost overcome with admiring congratulations. The coach had announced in the beginning that Elsie's sudden loss of voice had necessitated a substitute. The substitute, she added, was not exactly an understudy, but an innocent bystander with a phenomenal memory and real acting talent.

Since Pa and Ma were not there, it was a comfort to have Miss Marthann give her a squeeze and say, "Oh, my, Emmy, I didn't know you had it in you."

Mr. Carter said, "Where are your eyes, Miss Marty? This young lady's got everything. And pretty as a kitten besides."

Phil's funny voice, not entirely settled, muttered as if involuntarily, "She's not a kitten, Pop: she's a young aspen tree."

Emmy's quick incredulous glance caught Phil's flush at his own words. She also saw Abbie, dark-lashed eyes wide, twitch his sleeve and pout up at him. More, she saw Phil swing round and go off with Abbie, as if after all he didn't want to identify himself as the friend of a Lane; not before so many witnesses.

He likes me, yes; but he's ashamed of me. Oh, maybe he wouldn't have let it make a difference, if it hadn't been for that long-ago tantrum. Now he always thinks, she's pretty, and she's smart, but she's trash.

Though she kept on smiling as she talked to people, she watched his straight back and fair head move away from her, with Abbie's confiding blond waves too close to his shoulder. Maybe this was Emmy's last sight of him before they were grown up and settled for life.

But I don't really care, I don't really care, she told herself fiercely, pushing her curls back from her hot face and making herself smile and chatter with the people who were congratulating her.

She had told no one but Miss Marthann that they would be gone the next day, and she told no one now. It seemed less painful to slip away without anyone's knowing.

12

It Couldn't Happen to Me

THIS TIME the Lanes had more than usual to store in the truck, and Pa threatened to chuck out all the junk and leave it. Yet they were so practiced in packing and unpacking that they were ready by sunup.

Emmy paused in shaking down the ashes in the monkey stove to draw a deep breath of the frosty air. It tasted different from any other place or any other time of day. The water in the bucket had a thin coating of ice that shivered into tinkling bits as she tipped it over the ashes. Pa had taught them never to leave their campfire undrenched, even when, as now, it could hardly set fire to anything, there in the hard-trodden rectangle where the tent had stood these past months.

By the time they had established themselves in the loaded truck, Glen Lake was only beginning to waken, with no one in sight, and smoke rising from only a few chimneys.

"Truck sure ought to rouse them up," Pa said, as it went hiccuping and roaring down the road.

At least one person heard and recognized it. When it reached the Little Log Church, the door of the parsonage flew open, and Miss Marthann ran out, shrugging on a coat against the chill, and carefully holding before her a large box. Pa jammed on the brakes and brought the truck to a squalling stop.

"Well, my friends, you certainly are the early birds," her soft high voice greeted them. "I'm just eating breakfast. Won't you stop for another cup of coffee to warm you up?"

Pa said, "Thank you kindly, ma'am, but we got our work cut out for us if we're to make it to Californy before the jobs is gone. May be too late before we even start."

Regretfully Miss Marthann shook her head; understandingly she nodded it. "Just a little something for your lunch," she said, holding the box up to Pa. "Baked brownies yesterday. Too many for me. Do hurry back. It's been grand having Emmy and Chad around this fall."

The idling engine coughed and rumbled, coughed and took hold, while Pa grinned, Ma smiled faintly, Emmy and Chad waved. The parsonage dropped away behind them. Emmy looked back as they dipped toward the farmers' road, to wave once more, but the "preacher woman" was scudding through her yard and up the steps. Likely she'd heard the telephone, or remembered she'd left toast in the oven; but Emmy wished Miss Marthann had waited another minute at the gate, even if the toast did burn. This departure was sadder than most, and it would have helped to have the preacher waving at them till they were out of sight.

"It is too early to stop at the post office," Pa said. "Might be that Lucero kid would have another letter there; I don't know what else there'd be. And I take it you left a forwarding card, Emmy."

Emmy nodded. In the yard of Lil's little white house she could see the school bus waiting patiently, like a big yellow dog. Tomorrow morning it would be busy again, carrying Glen Lake pupils, sixth grade through twelfth. Lil's muscular arms would be manipulating its wheel and gears, and Lil's hearty voice calling hellos and goodbyes. Other yellow buses would come from all points of the compass, from the Black Forest and the foothills, for the school district covered two hundred and fifty square miles. The course of the buses would mark out the spokes of a wheel, with Obelisk the hub.

And Emmy and Chad would be far beyond the rim of that busy wheel.

Pa was tooling the truck to the left, to the farmers' road that wound up and down and around for some twenty miles before it came out on Highway 85. Pa claimed that he took this route only because of a little draw where the willows grew thick. He never admitted that he liked it for itself. In one place, where a rocky spine reached toward the road like a prehistoric reptile, Pa long ago had taken the children to find gypsum, beautiful crystalline chunks that glistened like pink taffy. Here, too, he had killed a rattlesnake. He looked from right to left in a pleased way, as if inspecting his own property. "If only it was deer season — " he muttered.

When they approached a knoll crowned with rocks like monstrous toadstools, he said thoughtfully that if he ever got back east again he'd relish some of the mushrooms they used to find through Indiana — the long, spongy kind.

Here and there farmhouses topped the heights, nestled

in hollows or sprawled on the slopes, like animals taking the morning sun, but they were few. It was a surprise, therefore, to see a man step into the road, his coat collar turned up against the early chill, his thumb jerked in the direction the Lanes were taking.

"By jinks, I never seen him ahead of us. Wonder where the dickens he sprung from?" Pa exclaimed, jamming on the brakes and bringing the truck to a screeching stop beyond the hitchhiker.

Emmy said, "Pa, isn't there a law in this state against picking up hitchhikers?"

She should have remembered how set Pa was against any interference with his liberty of action. He stared back at her, brows sardonic. "So? Since when has the law got a right to say who I can take in my own car, missy?"

By this time the stranger had hurried up, at a bias gait as if he had to look all ways at once. "Thanks," he said, pulling himself up over the tailboard and settling down beside Emmy, who drew a little away.

The truck went through its usual routine of coughing and jerking, but the engine would not turn over. Pa and Chad both tried their hand at it, but minutes passed, and the air was heavy with gasoline fumes before the starter caught and the vehicle started. During the delay the new passenger was tense and jittery, and even after they had picked up speed he glanced back, glanced ahead, stiffened whenever the motor stuttered. Emmy did not like the hard stare of his eyes out of his sallow, crooked face. Yet she had no forecast of the thing that happened when Pa drew the truck to a stop near Willow Run.

The stranger barked, "I wouldn't stop if I was you, mister."

Pa jerked around, unbelieving. "What's that you say?"

"You heard me. Drive right along. Unless you want a hole drilled through your middle." He was speaking straight and hard. "Head for the Black Forest, fast as this old heap can make it. Step on it. I got shells enough for the four of you. And for any nosy fool who tries to stop us."

Pa's head turned slowly, stiffly, to the front again, his shocked eyes touching Emmy's face in passing. The truck gathered speed. Ma sat slumped beside Pa and Chad next to Ma, all three as still as if they were statues of themselves. Emmy thought, This can't be happening. It does happen in the papers. But not to us.

The truck was making more speed than Emmy had supposed it could, jouncing crazily from side to side.

"Have to make such a racket?" the hitchhiker snarled. "Aiming to get picked up by the Sedalia police? Get wise, brother. I got nothing to lose. Don't know but I'd better rub you out right now and drive this heap myself. Oh-oh!"

He was peering back along the road at a horse and rider that had rounded a bend and were galloping after them. It couldn't be — but it was. It was Star, and Phil astride her, the little black dog far behind. Phil was waving as he came.

"Listen!" the stranger hissed. "I know you don't live hereabouts — chose you for your California license. But if you happen to know this gink, you okay anything I say. And make it good, sister." His narrowed eyes were menacing.

Watching the blue glint of the ugly little gun in his hand, Emmy wetted her dry lips. She could say nothing. Phil had come up within a few yards of the truck and was yelling at her.

"Emmy! A fine thing! Why couldn't you tell a guy? If it hadn't been for Miss Marthann's telephoning Mom — and my knowing a short cut — "

Phil paused for lack of breath, and the stranger's left hand caught Emmy's in a punishing grip. "Say something," he ordered without moving his lips.

"Hi, Phil." It was all Emmy could get out.

"You're not mad!" Phil protested, staring. He had not seemed to notice the hitchhiker before, but now he looked at him, blue-gray eyes intent.

"This a friend of yours, Amy?" the man asked in a tone heavily jocular. "I'm Amy's uncle from Missouri, ain't I, Amy?"

His fingernails bit into her arm, and without looking she could see the gun in his other hand, half hidden by the overlarge topcoat. She licked her lips and stretched them into a smile. "Oh, sure, Phil, this is my uncle. Surest thing you know, Phil. S-surest thing you know."

The stranger's grip relaxed.

Phil said, "Well, goodbye now, *Amy*. I didn't want you to get away without a goodbye and good wishes. Bye, Mrs. Lane — Mr. Lane. So long, Chad." Already he was wheeling around, and his final words were almost lost. "I'm in a tearing hurry, Amy, and — " He dug his knees into Star's sides and was off.

He had been too quick. Even without the twice stressed "Amy," Emmy would have known that he grasped the situation. The hitchhiker evidently knew, too.

"Wisenheimer!" he snarled. "Too smart for his breeches." Lifting his gun he sent a bullet screeching after horse and rider. To Emmy's horror, Phil seemed to sway in his saddle. Or had he only jerked when the bullet whizzed past? And could he possibly do anything to save them?

"Give her the gas," the stranger ordered, breathing hard. "Get us to the Black Forest, bud, if you want to see tomorrow. And no tricks."

Five more miles to Sedalia. Even this racketing, rocketing truck would make it in ten minutes. As Emmy gripped the side to steady herself and to keep as far as possible from the stranger her thoughts were careening like the truck. Ten minutes. Could Phil reach that nearest farmhouse, high on the hillside, telephone to the Sedalia police, get them alerted in time? Her eyes and ears strained to catch any sign of help. With sick certainty she knew what this man would do if they reached the Black Forest.

Over a narrow old wooden bridge — down into the

ditch in a detour where a new bridge was building — past huge orange-painted monsters of road machinery, with no one yet manning them — past a white house Emmy knew, and a man staring at them from the gate — up a slope and banging over railroad tracks and past a few stores — Sedalia.

No police car. No motorcycle cop. Emmy's hope died.

Wheels squalling, the truck turned south on Highway 85. It fled toward a road that angled east to the blot on the horizon, the Black Forest. There a criminal could easily hide, after doing away with anyone who might hinder him. On and on southward, the truck swaying with its speed —

Emmy's heart lurched. A hundred yards ahead, drawn up across the pavement, a police car — Shrieking up from behind, a motorcycle cop, crouching low in the saddle —

The hitchhiker looked forward, looked back, spat out ugly words. *Now if I could kick his hand — kick the gun away* — But Emmy could not move.

The hitchhiker was firing at the motorcycle. The officer returned his fire. The stranger was reaching for Emmy, snarling, "You can take this, sister, and — " His words broke off. He grabbed at his breast, the gun rattling from his clutch. When the truck had screeched to a stop, the stranger lay crumpled on the floor of the truck.

After that, things happened like a blurred movie. Ma slumped in a faint against Pa's shoulder. Chad clambered down from the truck. More officers raced up in a squad car, siren screaming.

Questions followed, and answers. "You folks sure got luck," a policeman told them, shaking a solemn head. "This guy was wanted bad. The Crab, they called him. Armed robbery. Murder. Wouldn't have stopped at anything."

Was wanted; wouldn't have: past tense. Emmy shuddered away from that still form beside her. "You mean he's — ?"

"Yeh, he's done, young lady. Cheated the chair."

The rest of the morning was an endless repetition of the same questions and answers, in the little police station, the Lanes too spent by their strange adventure to grow impatient.

Emmy did ask timidly for word of Phil, but without satisfaction until an officer turned smilingly from a telephone conversation and said, "That was the kid you asked about, miss, the one who turned in the alarm. Hard to convince him you folks were okay. Asked me three times."

"But was he all right himself?" Emmy asked breathlessly.

"Said if you inquired I was to say he was okay. Bullet just creased his upper arm. Said he was going to Castle Rock to have the doctor dress it, and he'd come by here. Seems to want to see for himself that you're all alive and kicking."

Pa asked, "How long you reckon we got to be held up here?"

"Well, there's the inquest, and of course you're the star witnesses. You and this young man from Glen Lake."

"Might as well make camp, then." Pa spoke quietly, as if all the bluster had been shaken out of him.

Before noon their simple housekeeping arrangements were established. The townspeople were attentive to them, as if they were heroes. The village, a handful of buildings scattered across the tracks and along the highway, had seldom made the radio broadcasts, and was enjoying the prospect. One woman came to tell them she had a good stove in her barn, and they were welcome to use it while they were detained: it must seem cold to California folks. This time the California license plate was playing a more agreeable part in the Lanes' affairs.

It was midafternoon when the Carters' green coupé slid to a stop before the Lanes' tent and Phil came tumbling out of the rear seat, his eyes so anxiously fixed on Emmy that he almost sprawled over a stone. Their questions burst out in unison:

"Emmy, you really all right?"

"Oh, Phil! What did the doctor say?"

Answers also were a swift duet:

"Oh, fine, thanks to you and Star."

"Doctor said okay. Lost a little blood is all."

Emmy turned to Phil's father and mother, who had followed him out of the car. Mrs. Carter was smiling down at Ma.

"Next time I won't take no for an answer, Sue Bingham," she scolded gently. "I won't let you get away again without a good visit."

"Mrs. Carter, it really was only a flesh wound?" Emmy appealed to her. "But imagine if he hadn't happened along!"

"Happened! That was no happenstance. When Miss Marty telephoned — seeing you pass us up without stopping — this young man tore out and saddled Star in two jerks of a lamb's tail — "

"But if I hadn't known a short cut — and you hadn't been so brave, Emmy Lane — " Phil put in.

"And if Lil Tudor hadn't given us a good code word — " Emmy was laughing, but her eyes still studied Phil's face and she burst out, "Phil, would you have guessed, if it hadn't been for the 'Amy' and the 'Surest thing you know'? Oh, Phil, we just owe everything to you."

"Well, I'd seen this guy's picture in the post office — I've always looked at those pictures, such ugly mugs, most of them — but I wasn't sure. As for owing, you think too much about what you owe folks, Emmy." Phil's face was working, and he scowled violently, as if to yank it back into shape. "You don't owe me a thing, any more than you do your Spanish Cavalier. But there's one thing," he hastened on, "you could promise to give up this silly notion of quitting school, you, of all people. You could promise you'd finish high school, wherever you were."

Emmy said, "We-ell — " while she thought, Miss Marthann must have told him why I feel bound to Andrés.

"Promise?"

Emmy looked at Pa and Ma, sitting on boxes before the tent. Pa tilted his hat forward, settled it back. "Crazy waste not to, Emmy, and you so far along. S'pose you ever needed to support yoreself? High school diploma'd give you a better chance at a job."

"Promise?" Phil repeated.

"I — promise, Phil." She didn't know whether to be glad or sorry.

Mrs. Carter was nodding, her warm brown eyes smiling. "Phil, remember doctor's orders: home and horizontal the rest of the day. Goodbye, Sue!"

Pa got to his feet, hat in hand, and made a little bow to Mrs. Carter. "Ma'am, like Emmy says, us Lanes owe everything to that boy of yores, and all our lives we'll be thanking him. Phil, you ain't no slouch for looks, but I got to say right now you ain't no sissy, neither." Pa, too, must have been remembering That Day.

"It wasn't so much, Mr. Lane," Phil mumbled, flushing as he glanced at Emmy. "Jiminy, I sure wished I could rope that guy with my lariat and jerk him out of the truck — away from Emmy. Only if I'd missed — "

"I'm thankful you didn't try that, bub."

The Carters drove back to Glen Lake, and the Lanes

settled down to make the best of the delay. Pa and Chad returned to the farmers' road and Willow Run and gathered materials as if the place had not been the scene of a grim drama that day.

While they awaited the inquest, the whole family worked on baskets. News photographers visited the tent and took pictures of them all, but especially of Emmy. And not only the townspeople came to see the Lanes, but others from miles away.

Pa said, "Looks like we could easy sell all the baskets we could make and then some. One lady asked me to autograph the one she bought, can you feature that? Know what? Us Lanes is famous."

On the day of Phil's second visit, Emmy stopped weaving baskets long enough to go to the big Castle Rock high school in his green coupé. There she got assignments from interested teachers, and bought secondhand books, so that she could get to work without more delay.

The inquest brought larger crowds, more reporters, more photographers, who seemed endlessly interested in pictures of Emmy and Phil; but at last the business was completed. The Lanes speedily dismantled their tent and took back the borrowed stove. The hour for goodbyes had come. Phil and Emmy leaned against the truck and found nothing to say.

At last Pa twisted around in the seat, where he had been pottering with invisible machinery, and said to Phil, "Sure hate to rush you off, bub, but we got to pull out. Wasted a week as it is."

Thus urged, Phil took Emmy's hand in an awkward grasp. "You mind your promise, Emmy Lou."

Mutely Emmy nodded.

"And, look: remember you don't owe anything, not anything, to that Lucero guy. Or to me, either, except just to finish high."

Pa was starting the motor. Above its noisy clatter Phil spoke quickly. "Well, goodbye. And I'll never forget you, Emmy, no matter what."

Emmy pulled herself up into the truck bed and they rattled away. Phil stood beside the coupé and waved until they went around a bend and lost him from sight.

"You don't owe anything to that Lucero guy . . . nor to me, either . . . I'll never forget you, no matter what . . . no matter what." Emmy repeated Phil's words over and over to herself. Their finality told her plainly that he, too, had been reinforcing old decisions.

He liked her, maybe as much as she liked him. Emmy could not fail to see his liking. Even her family's gypsy life might not have made her seem unworthy, especially since Pa's and Ma's people had been decent and respectable. But in combination with Emmy's uncontrollable temper —

Emmy blinked back the forbidden tears, squared her shoulders, stiffened her spine. This deep, hard ache was mere sentimentality. And she could not afford to be soft, for she had her work cut out for her, this year and next. It would not be easy to keep up with her classes when she wasn't in school, or even when she was in a half dozen different ones, all at different stages of progress. But she had given her word.

In spite of the aching lonesomeness, it was a comfort to have given her word, and to be forced to go to school again.

13

Round and Round and Round

THE JOURNEY to Conchita seemed longer than usual because of the Lanes' hurry to get there before all the good jobs were gone. It was actually longer, for the truck had never balked so often or required so many repairs.

"She never acted up like this, not in the last twenty years," Pa fumed. He always spoke as if the succession of trucks were a single vehicle. "And of all times for her to pick. She wouldn't quit on the farmers' road, like I was begging her to."

"If she had of, we'd be dead and buried," Chad said solemnly.

"Well, you may be right at that."

As the Lanes went hitching along, Emmy thought oftener of the Luceros than of the job ahead. She would be sitting in the back of the truck, head bent over a book, and Andrés's black eyes would be facing her. Emmy tried to focus on those ardent dark eyes, hoping that they would crowd out the wide-set blue-gray ones that were even more persistent.

And when the Lane truck pulled into the Conchita

camp one evening, the Luceros' were the first familiar faces they saw. With the old cries of welcome, the laughter, the embraces of Mrs. Lucero and all her daughters, the Luceros swarmed around the newcomers.

"Refugio, you're prettier than ever!" Emmy exclaimed, holding her off for a good look. Year by year Refugio grew more immaculate in her grooming, every lustrous lock of hair in place. Year by year she bloomed more richly, while prettier clothes set off her child-slim body.

She widened her eyes at Emmy. "You sure look more pretty, too, and more grown-up. Let me fix your hair like mine, no? Natural curly, what wouldn't I give for it!"

Andrés was looking soberly over his sister's head. "Mean to say it ain't even a year you been gone? Emmy, it's been a hundred. And how about the young Anglo in the newspaper pictures with you, Emmy? How about him?"

"Phil?" Emmy knew her tone was too casual. "I've known Phil since I was eight."

"You've known me longer'n that," Andrés retorted.

"Andrés, we better get this straight to start with. There's just one thing Phil Carter ever asked me, and that was not to stop school till I'd finished high. I promised that. I couldn't very well refuse, after he likely saved all our lives."

Andrés scowled blackly. "What's it to him if you finish high school or not? He's got his nerve. And, gosh, Emmy, is that another year? Or two?"

Afterward Emmy and Refugio had a long girl-to-girl talk with brothers shooed out of the way. Refugio marveled at Emmy's collection of news pictures. The California paper had carried only the one of Emmy and Phil together, and Andrés had torn the Luceros' copy into bits, because Emmy was smiling at Phil.

"Those photographers all told us just how to stand and just how to look," Emmy explained.

Refugio turned her shining black head this way and that, studying the different views of Phil. "He's awful spindly — *delgado*." Her tone was critical. "The neck is very-very long, no?"

Coldly Emmy replied that she hadn't noticed anything wrong with the neck. "He never takes a good picture."

"Not a patch on Andrés, even if Andrés is my brother. I'm sure glad you wasn't no later getting back."

"How do you mean?" Emmy thought there was significance in her friend's tone.

"Oh, nothing much. Only that Eufemia Martinez. Remember Eufemia? Red hair and these green eyes. Sure pretty, if that's the kind you like. No, listen!" — she waved vigorously to stop Emmy's interruption — "Don't you go blaming Andrés. He hasn't been no more than polite. But if a girl ever made a dead set at a fellow — It won't be nothing for you to cut her out, Emmy, now you're here. And it might help you to forget this Anglo kid," she added shrewdly.

Emmy was not destined to remain on the ground and

protect her proprietary interests. All the job openings in the Conchita camp had been filled during the long delay. Next day the Lanes made their adieus to the Luceros and went farther south in the Valley, where signs on the road as they came through had indicated that workers were still needed.

Emmy was both relieved and sorry to find that they must go too far from Conchita for Andrés to visit them often. He was paying for his jeep, and necessity kept him steadily at his job. Several Sundays the jeep came darting along the highway like a waterbug on a stream, bringing Andrés alone, or Andrés and Refugio. Once it brought a third passenger, Eufemia. Emmy eyed Eufemia's hair askance. How could any man prefer common black curls, she wondered, to that glowing nimbus, coppery, bronze, gold, almost purple, according to the light? How could he be immune to those strange gray-green eyes with their sweeping lashes? Yet Andrés ignored the Spanish girl completely, once he was within Emmy's orbit.

Since they were near enough for these occasional visits, Emmy and Andrés exchanged no letters. Now and then Emmy had a card from Phil, now and then a letter from Miss Marthann. The "preacher woman" no longer included newsletters. Emmy suspected it was because Abbie's name was so often linked with Phil's in the young peoples' activities. Again and again she reminded herself that she didn't care in the least. What she needed to worry about was her own affair, Eufemia and Andrés, in short.

Yet she was sure she could bring Andrés running by a crook of her little finger, no matter who might be hanging to his coattails.

Moreover, until she had made her difficult way through high school, she was better off without any boys around. There was no denying that boys were a distraction.

For two months the Lanes worked in the citrus. Here Emmy added a particularly good school to her collection. Here also she added a Christmas celebration.

The wandering Lanes had never made much of Christmas. As a child the holiday decorations in towns and cities had fascinated Emmy, especially the lighted trees in house windows. Vaguely, as one might wish to be a part of fairyland, she had wished that she might be part of a house like those.

The camp where they were now stopping was not so good as the one at Conchita. It had no showers, no laundries, and only a few primitive outhouses. But a few days before Christmas a strange-looking truck made its way slowly into an open space amid the camp shacks and tents. It carried a decked Christmas tree, and at nightfall its lights, plugged into an office outlet, sparkled and shone like jewels.

Surprisingly, Ma shrugged into her sweater and folded a scarf over her head as soon as Emmy had washed the supper dishes. Pa looked at her questioningly. "You feel up to a walk, Ma? Or what?"

"Christmas," Ma quavered. "It's been — years — "

Pa scowled his unwillingness, but he pulled on the felt hat that was his outdoor costume and went with her, and Chad and Emmy trailed after them.

"In Glen Lake they have big doings," Emmy said to Chad. "I always kind of hoped — Miss Marthann and an English woman who lived there, they worked out a Yule Log Festival, the way folks had it in old-time England. And they have that star, bigger than a city block, lighted on the hill at night. And on the day itself folks come for miles, hundreds of folks, and they go and hunt the log that's been hidden in the hills, and the fellow who finds it gets to ride it down to the Town Hall — "

Here in camp the celebration consisted of colored slides of the Christmas story, thrown on the side of a company building, and Christmas carols led by a voice over a loud-speaker. Emmy heard a small, choking sound from Ma, and looked at her in quick alarm. Unheard-of tears were sliding down Ma's cheeks.

Pa got tired of the citrus fruits; couldn't abide the smell any longer, nor the sting on his hands. So they moved on to the dates. It was not harvest time, but there was plenty of pruning to do, and a shortage of labor for it. Pa had picked up this skill also. Pa could do anything he set his mind to, Emmy thought with a sigh.

Emmy found another good school nearby, and with less work to do she had more time for study. She loved the palm groves, their exotic fronds forming great, perfect arches. Each year lifted the fruit higher, so that platforms were built around the trunk farther and farther up, for the handwork that was vital to the crop. Pa even knew just how to pollinate the long blossom-clusters, all the pollination being done by hand. It was wet work, in the groves, since date palms need to stand in the water with their heads in the sun. But it was a change, and by the time the seasonal work slump reached the dates, Pa was willing to return to the citrus grove, this time to the oranges.

That spring they made their way with maddening slowness toward Colorado, taking the northerly route and stopping in Fort Lupton for a job in the beets. The Luceros were not there that season, and without them Emmy felt freer to work and study. Yet she missed Refugio, and she missed Andrés. His unquestioning devotion was a tonic.

Or was it a sleeping pill?

It was the end of August when Pa grew tired of the potatoes and peas that followed the beets, and started the truck southward. They were headed for California, he said with emphasis. Emmy knew how he must feel: afraid that Emmy and Miss Marthann between them might pull the strings to keep them awhile at Glen Lake. As soon as they approached the town he began to twitch like a horse that feels the sting of flies.

So here she was, Emmy Lane, almost eighteen, maneuvering the old truck up and down the hilly roads between

Denver and the Glen while Pa drowsed in the truck bed, his dreary old hat tilted over his eyes. Same kind of truck same roads, same Emmy, same fear. No, not quite the same fear. One after another the doors had opened when she knocked. But the final one —

She felt that final door jarring shut when Pa roused himself with a shuddering yawn and sat up to look around him. Instinct must have wakened him, for they were nearing the point where the farmers' road led off toward the Glen. Without glancing back, Emmy could feel that Pa was blinking around him.

"Hey!" he rumbled, still husky with sleep, "If we go to the Glen to pick up any mail, I want it understood that we ain't stopping all winter. Get that, missy? Post office, yes. Might get news about jobs at Conchita."

Ma had been sitting at Emmy's side, with Chad beyond her. She spoke out of one of her heavy silences. "Pa — not without stopping. At the cemetery. And the old home place — to see if the irises and tulips bloomed."

Pa grunted. "Irises and tulips in August, Ma?"

Ma's voice trembled. "The seed pods would tell — "

Again Pa grunted. But Ma had shown so little interest lately that he was evidently unable to deny her. "Well," he conceded.

Emmy turned the truck to the right, down the hill and across the tracks to the farmers' road. Though she sternly reminded herself that this would be no more than a tantalizing glimpse, her heart was beating fast when at last they came into the wide place in the road where most of Glen Lake's business was centered.

Trucks and jalopies, automobiles shabby and sleek, were nosing in around the little post office. Some were town cars, with Denver's county numeral 1, or Colorado Springs' 4, or out-of-state licenses, for vacation would not be over till Labor Day.

"Must be the mail's just in," Pa said, squinting from sun to waiting people. "Me and Chad can pick up some grub while you ask for mail, Emmy. Too late to go on to the burying-ground tonight."

While Ma made herself small on the truck seat, and Pa and Chad went into the grocery store, Emmy drew a deep breath and entered the post office. Her mind was empty. All she felt was a dizziness that made it hard for her to breathe. Altitude, she scornfully told herself.

The small lobby was crammed with people waiting for the mail to be sorted. Elsie Babcock was the first to see Emmy, and even as she met her with cries of welcome, Lil came striding in, her big smile ready, her greetings flowing from side to side.

"Hi!" she greeted Emmy warmly. "Are you the gal I'm sorry to see! Surest thing you know!" She overflowed with pleased laughter.

Evidently the phrase had become a part of Glen Lake's vocabulary. Evidently, too, Lil accepted it as a tribute. Even the summer people were acquainted with it, judging by the appreciative ripple that ran through the packed group. The postmistress paused in sorting the mail to peer out and grin at Emmy. Emmy felt almost as she had on the school stage, months earlier. She was relieved when the tight clusters parted and let Miss Marthann through.

"Well, if it isn't Emmy Lane! I've been on the lookout for you all summer. You're just in good time to start your senior year."

Shaking her head, Emmy found words after the moments of mute embarrassment. "Reckon I'll have to get that senior year catch as catch can. California, Pa says."

Miss Marthann's eyes clouded, but she only said, "Well. Soon as we get our mail I'll go out and see your father and mother. And Chad. Emmy, I like that boy. You don't realize at first how much there is to him, because of the way he burns his own smoke."

By the time the mail was all out and Miss Marthann had got a stack from her box and Emmy one piece from the window, Pa and Chad were back in the truck with Ma, waiting.

"Good to see you!" Miss Marthann called warmly. "Aren't you going to settle down with us awhile?"

Pa lifted his hat to scratch his head, and then thought to lay the hat on his knee instead of replacing it. "Seems like we got to be getting on, ma'am. Only reason we looped round by the Glen was to get any mail might have come. And so the wife could kindy see to the family graves."

Miss Marthann's brow puckered, but she made no protest. "I'll see you tomorrow, anyway," she said, waving them on their way.

The sun had dipped behind the western mountain when they chugged up the road into the clearing. The minute that sun was gone, even now while summer still lingered, a sweet coolness replaced the bland warmth.

Ma said, as if the words were pulled out of her, "Feels like — like a cold drink. When you're parched dry."

Chad was out of the truck before it stopped, and racing round the clearing. "Wind never got her!" he crowed, an exultant hand on the chimney of his barbecue fireplace.

"Looks like the little stove ain't too bad rusted to cook us one meal, or two," Pa mused.

Ma said, "Roses."

"And look, Ma," Emmy called. "The marigolds must

have seeded themselves. They're little, but aren't they cheery?"

"Looky." Chad was pointing to the oblong of packed earth where their tent had stood so long. It still showed distinctly, and made this more like a real homecoming.

Pa and Chad set up the tent and lugged in the pallets. Emmy kindled a fire. She built it in the barbecue rather than in the tent, because the evening was so enchanting. When they drew their boxes round the fire to eat the quickly prepared supper, Emmy absently registered the fact that Pa had left the trunk in the car. At other times it would have fallen on her hopes like a physical blow, but now she had no hopes.

Pa was genial tonight. That was because she had not urged their staying here, Emmy thought. "Get any mail, Emmy?" he asked, when they had softened the sharp edge of their hunger and were more leisurely savoring the mulligan stew. "What with the preacher woman and all, I plumb forgot to ask you."

"Just one letter. For me. I haven't opened it yet."

Pa blew on a spoonful of the stew, which he had just dipped, scalding hot, from the kettle. "Who from?"

"Andrés."

Pa scowled slightly. "What's that punk got to say?"

Chad the silent grumbled, "Andrés ain't never got nothing to say."

Silently Emmy pulled the rumpled letter from her jeans pocket and opened it with a bobby pin. The writing was as untidy as ever, and the spelling as poor; but the sense was different.

When Emmy had read it through a second time, Pa asked impatiently, "Well? Likely he don't mention no jobs. Jobs wouldn't be important enough." His tone changed as Emmy lifted her eyes from the letter and stared blankly ahead. "What's the matter, girl? Read it off, can't you? Only leave out the mush."

Emmy moistened her lips and gulped. "There isn't any — any mush. He says, do I know how long it's been? He says, can I give him something to go on? You can't blame Andrés for feeling like that, Pa," she added faintly.

Her eyes went again down the lines of scrawled writing:

Understand, Emmy, theres noboddy like you. But a fellows got to have somebody. If you come back for the winter crops, youll find me waiting for you Emmy. But not much longer. Im going nuts.

Blindly Emmy stuffed the envelope back in her pocket. "He says if we come back for the winter harvest, okay, but he doesn't want to wait any longer than that."

Pa's genial mood had been swallowed up in blackness. Emmy didn't try to understand whether his pride was affronted by Andrés's ultimatum or by the necessity of admitting that the marriage of a Lane and a Lucero could be possible.

Silently the family sat for a while after supper was

eaten and the dishes washed. As so often before from this clearing, they watched the moon floating huge and rosy on the horizon, beyond the lake and over to the left of Ben Lomond. The crickets fiddled tirelessly, and unseen birds flew and called in the bushes.

"What's those birds that goes around crying like that?" Chad demanded indignantly.

"Grosbeaks," said Ma.

"Baby ones," Pa grunted.

To the west of the clearing the stalks of last summer's mullein and angelica — or was it really poison hemlock? — stood as before in miniature forests. But they were different. They drew away, as if the Lanes were intruders in the clearing.

Pa rose, stretched, yawned. "Mite chilly for me. Reckon I'll turn in."

They all went to bed, nobody saying anything more. For a long time Emmy lay listening to the crickets, and to the sound of the wind in the pines, and to the occasional hooting cry of an owl. She might not be here again. High school she must finish, yes, but she could do that in California and relieve Andrés's anxiety. It was high time for her to stop shillyshallying.

When she did sleep, she had a dream that had been several times repeated that year. She came to Glen Lake. She climbed to the Little Log Church and the parsonage, looking for just two things, the Carter house and Phil. And the house wasn't there. Phil wasn't there.

An angry shout from Pa roused her. "Emmy, wake up and quit bawling. When you going to grow up and quit yore sleep-talking? Yore ma's plumbed tuckered out and needs her rest."

As she drifted off again, Emmy heard him say, "Now, Sue. Now, Sue. It don't mean nothing. She ain't much more than a baby."

"Eighteen."

"But it was you who said what a good boy he was. Land knows it sticks in my craw to see a Lane take up with a furrin migrant — "

"Pa — with her so wrapped up in books — and houses — and him not — "

"Now, Sue!"

Pa's voice held the distress, the tenderness, which always disturbed Emmy. She covered her head with the lumpy old pillow, as usual, and had soon floundered back into her uneasy dreams.

14

Again Pa Decides

Miss Marthann appeared at the tent soon after breakfast. "Glad I got here before you'd left for the cemetery," she cried, breathless from hurry. "I've been dividing my tulip bulbs, and I've got too many; thought maybe you could use them in your lot: Red Emperor and Indian Chief and Copper Queen: they're all marked. Are you coming back here after you tend the graves, or going right out to the highway?" Her quick eyes seemed to be registering the fact that nothing had been done toward packing the truck.

Emmy, too, had noted Pa's unusual leisureliness in the matter. Yet his reply took her by surprise.

He pushed his hat forward, pushed it back, again remembered to take it off. "Don't happen to have any fresh jobs up yore sleeve?" His tone held so grim a drollery and his eye so dry a glint that Emmy thought for a moment that he might be teasing Miss Marthann. His next words corrected that idea, and sent Emmy's mouth open in dumb amazement. "I ain't talked it over with the wife yet, but

I got a notion she'd like to stay till snow flies. We been neglecting the baskets, and we could use the time to make up a supply of them if you hain't got no jobs in mind. And like enough Emmy could work part time in the rabbit place, like she did before, along with taking another turn in school."

When the incredulous silence prolonged itself, Pa added, awkwardly for him, "The wife's poorly, and it might do her a sight of good. More than that — " Now his words were meaningly deliberate — "it might do Emmy good, not to go back to Californy straight off."

By this time Miss Marthann was laughing with pleasure. "If you knew how much I've been wanting a couple of picnic sets made for the church lawn. And that's only a start, Mr. Lane."

Emmy had thought that she and Chad would never again stand in this chattering little crowd before the Jones store, waiting for the Obelisk school bus. She had thought they would never again hear Lil Tudor caroling her welcome from the driver's seat. Yet, incredibly, here they were, in the fragrant freshness of the mountain morning, Chad darkly smoldering, still so angry that he was trying to act as if he were no relation to his sister.

Emmy was still in the unreal world into which Pa's astonishing reversal had thrust her. For years the round of events had been unchanged. At every visit to Glen Lake Emmy had hung on for dear life, raging, pleading to

stay longer. At every visit Pa had relentlessly driven ahead, or reluctantly stopped for a little while, prolonging the stay if the "preacher woman wangled him into it." His voluntary offer to stay had sent Emmy off balance. It was as if she had tugged with all her might at a heavy-looking stone and found it had no weight at all. Besides, the delay would mean that she would lose Andrés, which was precisely what Pa hoped. Now there would be no use in answering his letter. And having no one — no one! — gave Emmy a lost, unanchored feeling in this unreal world.

"Well, now, this sure is a pleasure!" Lil said in her large, friendly way, as they waited for some latecomers running down the hilly street. "Sure glad you're going to have your senior year with us, Emmy. And you, Chad."

Emmy said, "It'll only be till winter sets in, Lil. My father's work — "

A small, cool voice broke in. "Your father's work is always taking you away, Emmy. Such a pity. But I never did get it clear in my mind what his business is." A smile was pasted on Abbie's soft little face, and her china-blue eyes blinked fast, as if she were deeply interested.

Looking at her perfectness of hair and skin and costume and hearing the neat precision of her syllables, Emmy felt the old wrath swelling within her. Phil — figuratively — stepped between the two.

"Mr. Lane's a very good carpenter," he said. "And cabinetmaker. Miss Marty thinks there's no one like him. And he's a sort of manufacturer — and retailer — "

Abbie's brows lifted. "Oh. Baskets."

Emmy had grown strangely tranquil. "Yes, baskets, Abbie. We make them and we peddle them. The best baskets anyone could want."

"You bet," Chad's growl echoed her.

The unpleasant moment had passed.

The Glen students were not alone in welcoming the brother and sister warmly. Angelo Baca, the handsome, serious boy from a Black Forest fox farm, lighted up at sight of Emmy. His racial characteristics were like those of Andrés, yet Emmy knew that even Ma would consider him suitable, since he was as bookish as Emmy herself, and since his family had a good home. It seemed strange that his open admiration did no more than soothe Emmy's pride. Chad's old teammates from sixth-grade football greeted him with a whoop. And one of the ranch girls from the foothills country to the east slid an arm across Emmy's shoulders and crowed, "Here's our next star! Anybody want to bet Emmy Lane won't get the fattest part in the senior play?"

"Oh, I'd love it," Emmy demurred hastily, "only we won't be here after winter sets in."

Many times during the next days she had to make the same reply.

Miss Freeman, the blue-eyed Home Ec teacher, stopped her after class to say, "Emmy, I've had inquiries from those letters you wrote to the bookstores in the Springs. Looks like you could get a Christmas job there if you wanted it."

"Oh, Miss Freeman, wouldn't it be heaven to work in a bookstore! But by Christmas we'll be in California."

The drama coach halted her in a corridor. "Glad you're back, Emmy Lane. I've got plans for you."

"Oh, I'd love it more than I can say, but — "

Yes, after all, Emmy's life went round and round and round.

The English teacher, the one they called Dr. Marian, because she had lately earned her Ph.D., beckoned Emmy to her desk at the close of a session. "Want to lend a hand with the school paper, Emmy? You express yourself well: nice, short crisp words. Moreover, you're not apathetic, like so many of today's teen-agers" — she shook an impatient head — "they act as if nothing is worth their while if it means an hour of work."

Catching her breath, Emmy answered, "But, Dr. Marian, how could my vocabulary be — ? With so many words I'm just beginning to get on to — "

"Maybe that's one reason for your vigorous style," the teacher said thoughtfully.

"But there's no telling how soon we'll go on. Depends on when snow flies, I reckon."

"Well, suppose you give us the benefit of your enthusiasm as long as you're here," Dr. Marian said, rapping a new class to order.

The climax came when Dr. Finch called Emmy as she passed the office door. She went in and stood balancing her books at the edge of his desk while she waited.

"What have you in mind after you're through here, Emmy?"

Emmy drew a long breath and shook her head. "Well, just to graduate from high school, sir — "

Studying her from shrewd, kind eyes, Mr. Finch finished her sentence in a way quite different from what she had meant. "I know. Exactly. Just to be graduated from high school may satisfy many students, but not you. Not with your ability and ambition. So this senior year we should be helping you shape your course more definitely toward what's coming next. Have you decided what major you would choose for college? And what college?"

College — college — Emmy pushed up against the desk to steady her suddenly shaking knees. Her gaze shifted over Mr. Finch's reddish aureole of hair, and out the window to the great expanse of plains, foothills, mountains, the dazzling sun, the rainbows that couldn't be there. When her giddiness had passed, she looked down again at the reddish hair flickering like a windblown flame, and at the quizzical face below it.

"Maybe Berea College," she stammered. "It's near where Pa — my father — was born and raised in Kentucky. Or Berry College in Georgia."

Emmy heard herself say this as if she were listening to someone else's words. Two minutes earlier she would have told you that Emmy Lou Lane had never once dreamed of college; and she would have believed that she was speaking the truth. And all the time Berea and Berry must have been waiting in a dim corner of her mind and memory, to pop out when she gave them a chance. They must have hidden there when first she heard of those institutions where students, even though their preparation was deficient, could work their way through. Now, as if her own words had released them, they were growing in size and reality.

Mr. Finch said, "You know, it might not be necessary to go as far away as all that. There are scholarships."

Emmy stared at him.

"Some scholarships pay only a little, or pay tuition for a year," he went on, tilting back in his swivel chair so that its springs twanged, and drumming the desk with his square-tipped fingers. "Others take the student right through the four years. Of course he has to find money for clothes, and for books and the like. Obelisk has only one big scholarship available in a state college, and naturally that goes to a most outstanding pupil."

Emmy was still unable to speak. She stood staring and unconsciously biting her lips.

Mr. Finch laughed, letting his chair spring forward with another loud complaint. "You stick by us, Emmy, and it might be you."

Emmy shook her head. "I'm — I'm not an extra-good scholar, sir. Phil Carter gets better grades. And Angelo Baca. And Abbie Allen," she added unwillingly. "Oh, heaps more kids."

Mr. Finch threw back his head and his green eyes went shut as he boomed his delight. "Maybe so. But show me six with half your go-getting quality, young lady. Or with your faculty for looking hard work in the face. Nowadays young people look at work the way a cat looks at water: go a mile around to avoid it." He sounded as disgusted as Dr. Marian had. "Well, think it over, Emmy Lane."

Of course it can never happen, Emmy said to herself. But just the thought is something I'll treasure all my life.

The joy of these weeks brightened instead of growing dull. When the senior class elected officers, they made Emmy historian, against all her protests. They refused to believe that she couldn't stay all year, and they insisted that they would have no one else as long as she was with them.

That autumn had the kind of weather Colorado claims as its normal sort. The nights were cold and clear, with a glitter of stars piercing the dark blue sky. Mornings and evenings were crisp as thin toast, middays hot-buttered with sunshine.

"This weather's like life, sort of," Emmy said to Phil on one of the rare mornings when they reached the bus stop ahead of their schoolmates.

Phil's eyes, as they studied her, had their curious, withholding gaze. "How do you mean?"

"Notice how peaceful, and sort of happy and good, the village looks. You'd think it could never get stirred up and stormy. Same way with this Indian summer. I know it will quit and let winter come, but I keep feeling as if it would last forever."

They were interrupted by Abbie's breathless little voice.

"Oh, Phil, I'm sorry I didn't hear you call to me. Isn't

it hot today?" She fanned herself with a soft small hand, tipped with rose-colored nails.

Emmy thought that no boy could help looking at her as Phil was looking now, with eyes almost hypnotized. In her summer dress she was as fragile and lovely as a sweet-pea. Emmy wondered if Phil had noticed how much she resembled her mother when she rounded her eyes so that the white showed all the way round, like blue china marbles. She wondered whether he noticed the droop of her soft little mouth when she forgot to keep it sweet. Maybe he did; right now his bemused look was edged with a puzzled questioning.

Even Abbie could not spoil those days for Emmy. Even the loss of both Phil and Andrés. For those autumn weeks were brimful of everything else Emmy wanted. She had all the books she could devour, at school and at the church library. She had the thrills of daily school life, of being part, if only for a little while, of this crowd of boys and girls who lived in settled houses. She belonged.

She had the new, exciting fun of helping get out the school paper. And she had her Saturdays of gainful work at the rabbit mills. She was working so hard that more than once she repeated her past experience of falling asleep while she studied back of the tent, the lantern lighting her work, a hot brick at her feet, and a quilt draped around her over her heaviest coat.

Pa had quickly made the picnic sets for Miss Marthann.

They were sturdy, compact affairs in two sections, each of which could be changed from a bench with a comfortable back to a bench with a narrow table. The Assembly people, seeing them on the church lawn, had ordered a number of them for their own grounds, and Pa was working, somewhat silently, on the new order.

Ma looked better, and some days had enough energy to potter around and make apple jelly and apple butter, a little at a time. She would not go to church, or even into the store. When anyone urged her, even Mrs. Carter, she reminded Emmy of a wild rabbit, sitting still as a stone, with only a look in the eyes to show its terror. When no one — except Miss Marthann — noticed her, she seemed content to be at the Glen.

So the Lane life went on placidly, and it was mid-October before the weather changed it. The day had been unseasonably warm, and Pa had studied the sky, shaking his head as he held out a wetted finger to catch any breeze.

"Weather-breeder," he said.

Emmy hurried her washing out on the tent ropes and bushes before she went to school, for it had not dried yesterday afternoon. "Would you fetch it in if a storm blew up?" she asked, eyeing her mother uncertainly.

The day passed beamingly, however, and when Emmy got home she brought in the clothes, dry and sweet-smelling. Perhaps Pa's forecast was wrong. In the night she roused once and heard him stuffing the monkey stove with fuel, and found herself curled up so tight that her legs ached. As the heat from the stove reached her, she uncurled enough to sleep again, without thinking what the sharp chill might mean to her happiness. In the morning came full realization.

"Emmy! Hey, Emmy? Guess what! Snow!" It was Chad, who had rarely seen snow.

Emmy sat up and blinked. Pa was already dressed and shaking down the stove. The quality of light in the tent was different, and the quality of stillness. Triumphantly, like a salesman displaying a new model, Chad held open the tent flap. Fluffy whiteness blanketed the world, and a few flakes still drifted in the air. Emmy reached for her clothes and dressed under the covers, her heart heavy.

The family breakfasted in the stuffiness of the tent, though Chad had swept a clear space beside the barbecue, and coaxed them to eat outdoors. Pa drank his coffee scalding hot, holding his other hand to the fire.

"Brrrr!" he shivered. "Sure glad we're pulling out."

"Pa," Ma said, "weather's prettiest after the first freeze."

"So I've heard. Time and again. Time and time and time again," Pa answered dryly. "Though up to now it's always been Emmy that's begged to stay. I only hope you're right this time, Ma. It'll take us two days to finish up all them picnic do-dads. I'll be right glad if we get good weather for traveling day after tomorrow."

Day after tomorrow. Emmy left her half-eaten breakfast and went silently outside. The sun shone gloriously from beyond the lake and Ben Lomond. It turned this hillside facing it an ethereal pink. Farther up the hill—Emmy saw it unbelievingly—each tree and bush wore a shadow like a plaque of turquoise. The beauty and glory of the scene made Emmy ache. And this time there was no use appealing her case.

She and Chad were first to break the sparkling whiteness down to the traveled road, the fresh, sharp smell biting their nostrils as they trudged through it. Everyone but Emmy was excited by the snow, she thought heavily. Chad floundered from side to side, finding bird tracks and others that he was sure were deer's, but Emmy plodded ahead, unsmiling. At the bus stop the youngest students were washing each other's faces and cramming snow down each other's backs. Even the older boys made snowballs and wound up like baseball players to throw them, while the girls watched and giggled. Abbie was cuddled in a coat the color of a morning-glory. It made her look like an angel, Emmy thought with pain.

"Isn't the world like a great big cake covered with seven-minute icing?" Elsie observed, blinking thoughtfully.

Abbie's baby voice inquired, "Know what it's really like? An ermine cloak. Wouldn't I love to have one!"

Phil said, "Reminds me of one of those sparkly frosted Christmas cards. What's it make you think of, Emmy?"

"California." Emmy hadn't been braced for the question, or for the tears that stung her nose, but nobody seemed to notice the tremble in her voice. They laughed at the joke, only Phil tacking a questioning frown to his laughter.

It seemed ironic that this was freshman initiation day, with dozens of boys and girls in fantastic make-up and costume. Not until after school, when Emmy stayed to help with the paper, did she express her feelings about the masquerade.

It was a time and place that encouraged emotion and the flow of thought. The big school was quiet now, except for yells from the athletic field — already cleared of snow and steaming in the sun — the bump of floor brushes and mops in the halls, and occasional racing, thumping feet on the stairs.

"All the clowns and babies we see on this Freshman Day," wrote Emmy, "seem to make an education something to laugh or cry about. Maybe the ones who can play their way through school are the lucky ones. Then again, maybe they aren't."

Phil also worked on the paper. Drawn perhaps by the fierce sprinting of Emmy's pencil, he stopped behind her and peered down over her shoulder. "Hi," he said, "not bad, Em. Only the clowns and babies may be sore at you."

"I'll be out of their reach," Emmy said.

Phil's voice was startled. "You don't mean — ?"

"I'll tell you on the way home."

The bus came back after the students who had regular after-school activities, and Lil greeted Emmy with concern as she clambered aboard, followed by Phil and a muddy, disheveled Chad, who had stayed for football practice.

"Emmy, you look like something the cat dragged in!" Lil cried. "Winter weather too much for your California blood?"

Emmy could manage nothing better than a shaky smile.

"Hey, Em, don't you like winter?" Phil protested.

"Sure I like it." Emmy sniffed and had to fumble for her handkerchief. "It's Pa that hates it. He says we have to go on day after tomorrow."

"No kidding? Gosh, I thought you'd be here for Christmas and the Yule Log, this time."

Emmy had got her eyes and nose under control. "It'll be all the same a hundred years from now," she said with false cheer.

"Well, now, I wouldn't say that." Phil's tone didn't quite manage to be facetious. "You know, Em, sometimes I wonder."

Blowing her nose again, Emmy eyed him questioningly, but he did not explain. Does he mean him and Abbie? she wondered. Does he mean me and Andrés? "I'm only thinking about — about school and how I've loved it this fall. Loved being part of it."

Phil nodded, frowning. "I know. The school paper and the class history and the senior play. And the scholarship — oh, oh, gosh, Emmy, that scholarship!"

Emmy forced a shaky laugh. "Kid stuff. All except

the scholarship and that was nothing but a dream anyway. But it's — it's immature to feel this way, as if school activities were the whole of life. Do you suppose real trouble can mean any more to us, Phil? I mean when we're settled and old?"

"Like when I couldn't go out for football — But look, Em, we're already here."

Slowly the three walked up the hill road, already dried by the day's hot sun. In the fields the tawny grasses rose golden from the fast settling snow. An occasional laden spruce let its white velvet mantle slip to the ground with a sighing rush. Emmy lifted her eyes to the white hill behind the church, where the great star would shine at Christmas.

The two were so absorbed in their talk that once or twice they stopped short to emphasize a point, and Chad blundered straight into them, maybe wrapped in thoughts of his own.

The second time it was Phil who brought them to a halt. "Look, Emmy! Didn't you have your eighteenth birthday this fall?"

She nodded. "Kept it quiet, because the other seniors are younger."

"Not me, having to stay out two years. But, look, Emmy! you're of age!"

She gaped at him.

Phil kicked at the snow along the edge of the road. "Sounds as if I was advising you to be a prodigal daughter," he blurted out, "but — why don't you just take things into your own hands, Emmy? Stay at the Glen till commencement?"

Emmy closed her mouth, swallowed, opened it to say, "You mean — you think I really could? Let Pa and Ma go on?"

"Pa and Ma and Chad," her brother's husky voice put in.

She had forgotten Chad. Now she looked down at him affectionately. At fifteen he had only begun to grow. "You and I would stay together and keep on at school, Chad," Emmy said. "Oh, Phil, it just doesn't seem possible."

Her incredulous joy in the possibility was unexpectedly shattered.

"No!" shouted Chad. He flung his books down in the road and stamped on them, while words came from him in stormy gusts. "You can stay in your old school, Emmy Lane. Not me. You're always trying to manage me. If it hadn't been for you, Pa never would have made me go to no school. Why can't you see? Me and Pa, we want to go places and see things, not be stuck in one place like bumps on a log. And books — I hate and despise 'em, and if — "

Incredulous fury was mounting to Emmy's brain. "Why, you — you — you — " she stuttered, and grabbed herself before hateful words could escape her. This time, as in the old days, she needed help to tame the storm, the rage, the tears. All her bright dreams were being jerked away from her, and this little ninny would spoil the chance for both of them. For Pa would never let her stay in the Glen alone.

Her books also dropped into the snow, as she gripped her hands behind her back and glared at Chad. Her head quivered with intensity and her neck muscles went taut; she didn't even notice that the old words were growing more audible as she repeated them: "The God in me salutes the God in you — "

A curious sound jerked her attention to Phil. He was snorting, and as she turned her eyes toward him, his tight-clamped mouth burst open in a helpless shout of laughter.

Emmy stood with hands still clasped behind her, and glared. "Seems like you wouldn't make fun — " Her voice was outraged.

"Honest I'm not making fun, Em." Phil's voice was soothing, his quirked fair brows at once indulgent and ironic. "But if you could only see yourself, so mad and so earnest — "

A sheepish smile twitched at Emmy's lips. Phil was looking at her as he had not since their childhood, with an appreciation that held nothing back.

"That routine of yours, Emmy, I saw it once before, and I thought, good gosh, is Emmy touched in the head? Oh, Em."

Chad had quieted, too, and stood poking at his books with his boot toe. "I don't care," he said sullenly. "I'm going with Pa."

Phil heaved a deep sigh and spoke normally. "Aren't we humans comical? Your father keeps you and your mother gypsying over the country when you both have a yen to settle and put down roots — when it's really hurt your mother not to. And here's Chad, who wants to roam, and you try to make him over in your own pattern."

Again Emmy stood staring and shaking her head. "No, you got it all wrong. About Ma, I mean. Ma hates houses. She's scared of folks. She — "

"Hates houses? That's not the way I heard it," said Phil. "Emmy, let's come on into the house and ask Mom what she thinks about all this."

"I'm going home," Chad broke in.

Phil's assent lacked regret. "Okay, kid. Tell your mother I'll walk Emmy home."

So Chad went splashing up the slushy road that branched off toward the clearing, and Emmy and Phil walked silently past church and parsonage to the Carter house.

1 5

The Shining World

ONLY ONCE BEFORE had Emmy entered the Carter house, and she looked quickly now to see if it was as wonderful as her memory of it. Yes; shabbier than she had remembered, but even more livable and gracious; and today permeated with the good fragrance of cooking apples and sugar.

The minute Phil poked his head into the door he began to shout in his young bass, "Mom! Hi, Mom! Where are you?" striding toward the kitchen where the spicy fruit smells were centered.

Mrs. Carter smiled at them from the stove, above the spoonful of apple butter which she was tilting sidewise to test. She was an apple-butter sort of woman, Emmy thought with a rush of feeling: ruddy brown from sunshine and the heat of the stove, and with a warm sweetness in her smile, a spicy keenness in her eyes, and a humor that could be tangy and sharp as cinnamon and cloves. Her graying dark hair curled softly in the heat. She was bonny, Emmy thought: the word didn't do her justice, but it was good as far as it went.

Automatically, Phil reached into a drawer for spoons, and handed one to Emmy. "Mom," he said, as he dipped

into a foamy saucer of preserve skimmings, "we have something important to talk over with you." He popped the spoon, upside down, into his mouth, like a little boy.

Mrs. Carter's eyes came quickly to her son's face, busy with the sweet mouthful. If she felt alarm at Phil's approach, she didn't show it. "Well, what is it now? Does a boy walk between two girls, or on the outside? Don't ask me. But I do know the latest football rules."

Phil waved his licked spoon, while Emmy's hung forgotten in her hand. Severely Phil said, "Come off, Mom, will you? This is serious. Don't you agree with me that it's time Emmy asserted herself?"

Mrs. Carter put down her ladle, folded her arms solidly across her crisp print apron, and looked resigned. "How about starting at the beginning? You know I'm not so smart as some folks I could name. Or anyway not as smart as they think they are."

"Well, Mr. Lane's set on traveling again. And, Mom, this girl's got Obelisk High eating out of her hand. It would be a crime for her to give it all up. Why, she'd have to start from scratch two or three times if she grabbed her senior year in two or three different high schools where nobody knew her. And, more than that, she'd be losing her chance at a scholarship. And here's the point, Mom. Emmy's eighteen, same as me."

Mrs. Carter's gravity seemed to deepen even as her interest quickened. She looked as if she were weighing many ideas. "Wouldn't your father be willing you and Chad should stay this one year, Emmy? Phil, get some cookies and milk for you and Emmy. Likely she hasn't your depraved appetite for preserve skimmings."

"But, ma'am, Chad is set against staying," Emmy said,

while Phil fished fragrant cookies from the jar and handed her two of them. "Mrs. Carter, it just doesn't seem possible. I know Chad's no hand for books, but — "

Waving away the cookies Phil was pressing upon her, Mrs. Carter considered Emmy. "Wouldn't your mother stay this winter, then? Let your father and Chad go on to California if they must?"

"Oh, that's another question I want Emmy to hear you answer," mumbled Phil, his mouth full of cooky. "Ask her, Em."

"Mrs. Carter, I can't take it in, what Phil says. He thinks Ma doesn't like to go gallivanting round the country, the way us Lanes have always done. But Ma always — Mrs. Carter, surely Phil's mixed up about this." Emmy fixed eager eyes on Mrs. Carter.

"What we women will do for our men! Maybe your mother has even made herself believe that way, Emmy. All I know really is what she was like to start with. Little Sue Bingham. My land, if you'd hunted the state over you couldn't have found a quieter little mouse, more of a mamma's girl." Mrs. Carter's brown eyes glowed as if smiling back across the years. "And pretty! There wasn't a girl in the Glen, or for miles around, that could hold a candle to her for looks. And she never seemed to know how pretty she was, with her shy, gentle ways: never made the most of herself."

"Boys like her?" inquired Phil, spooning preserves on a cooky already rich with nuts and raisins.

"Too shy with them. Didn't so much as have a date until your father came to town, Emmy. That was the winter she was sixteen. I was twelve, and I still remember the stir he made."

"The — stir?" Emmy asked wonderingly.

"Handsome!" Mrs. Carter shook her head in remembered admiration. "And such dashing ways! They all said he came from a good family, and showed it. All the girls made a set at him, but he didn't seem to take to folks. Didn't do more than smile and bow to any of the girls till he caught sight of Sue. I guess she was something different — And likely it was his being so different that broke down all the walls your mother had built up around herself. He wouldn't take no for an answer, and Sue surely didn't want to say no. It was a whirlwind courtship and as soon as she was seventeen a wedding in the Little Log Church, brand new then and with no Miss Marty. You never saw a more beautiful bride and groom."

"And she went off with Pa and never settled down again," Emmy said wonderingly, trying to straighten the story in her mind.

"My big sister was her bridesmaid; Phil's Aunt Meg. She used to say the only time Sue showed any uncertainty was just before Charlie took her away. Then she clung to Meg, begging her to look in on her parents sometimes. Said something incoherent about being scared to death to go off that way without any home, if it was anybody but Charlie."

For a while Phil and Emmy sat in the glossy-clean kitchen, nibbling cookies and sipping milk. Emmy hardly noticed what the others were saying, she was so busy making over her lifelong pictures of her family. The idea that Pa's folks were Somebodies had worn thin in her growing mind, but perhaps the careless years could have changed his manners as well as his grammar; perhaps, but Emmy still doubted it. As for Ma, the wall was still around her, and now she hid behind it in a way that had become frightening, would not even let Mrs. Carter inside. If the children had come early, Ma might have persuaded Pa to settle down. But it was ten years before Emmy was born, and probably by that time the pattern of their life had been set.

Emmy thought about many things she had always passed over: Ma's sympathy with her little girl's love for dolls and playhouses; her tenderness for the canary in its battered cage; her care for the blue glass slipper, which must have stood as a symbol of her sheltered girlhood. She recalled the way Ma always stared at unpainted shacks if they had clean windows and curtains and blossoming plants. Perhaps Ma had thought that such a shack might be in reach of her and Pa, if only Pa felt as she did. Had this roving existence really taken away Ma's will to live?

"But she always hated the nice painted houses." Emmy plumped the remark unmindfully into the middle of a conversation.

"Defense mechanism," said Phil.

Mrs. Carter went on ladling the rich brown butter into glass jars and smiling, as if at Emmy's absorption. "As we have been saying, Emmy, your parents might both be willing, just for this one year. After that it would be easier to arrange, with you in college."

Emmy widened her eyes. "College?" she said haltingly. "Willing?"

"You little goon," Phil scolded, "you haven't heard a word we were saying. Willing you and your mother should stay here until your father and Chad came back in the summer."

"You think we could make out in the tent?"

"Well, the tent's an item we'd have to figure on. But it certainly can't be too difficult. Why!" Mrs. Carter laughed delightedly, poising a spicy tablespoon over its jar. "Phil, what about that little bitty house the hermit used to have? I've heard your father say it was pretty sound. And it's on government land, so dear knows if anybody ever had a claim to it. It wouldn't be any great trick to move it up to the clearing — "

Another thought occurred to Emmy, as she sat fogged in a bright haze of happiness. "Mrs. Carter, did you say — college? For me?" She spatted her hand hard on her chest.

Phil laughed aloud, tilting back in his chair, and Mrs. Carter said, "Phil, will you ever learn? That ruins chairs. But, Emmy, why in this shining world shouldn't you go to college? You of all people?"

"If I can't stay here and get a scholarship like Mr. Finch said, maybe, why, I could go to Berea or Berry!" Suddenly Emmy knew she could. With all this warm confidence surrounding her, she could do anything in the shining world.

"No," Phil said decisively, "not to Berea or Berry, Em. I couldn't go to Berea, didn't you know that? Pop and Mom and I have had a college fund since I was knee-high to a duck. All my 4H project money's gone into it, and Pop and Mom's bonds. Berea won't take anybody who's got the wherewithal, and likely Berry's the same. So you've got to go to Aggies. With me."

Emmy looked quickly at Mrs. Carter, and saw the smile shrink once more. For a moment she studied Emmy gravely. It was as if she were contemplating a possibility and finding it not quite what she had hoped, yet not too bad.

"You would like Aggies, Emmy," she said at length. "I really think it's a fine idea."

The tension was relaxed by a sudden whoop of laughter from Phil, his released chair screeching an accompaniment.

"Now what?" his mother asked. "Phil, that chair!"

"Oh, I just remembered Emmy and her routine. Mind if I tell Mom about your incantations, Em?" He did not wait for her reply. "Mom, you remember my telling you about seeing this little goon go through a funny stunt once? Kind of worried me. Today I found out what it was. My gosh, Mom, she took old Selby seriously. She used that God-in-me business to get hold of her mad — "

"It works." Emmy's tone was half defiant. "My temper's never got the best of me, not since that time, Phil — "

Mrs. Carter spoke with the warm glow that was always in her eyes to soften her reproof of Phil. "My son, I must say I like Emmy's attitude better than yours. Poor Miss Selby, meaning every word, and you Glen hoodlums always laughing at her. Old Selby, indeed! Where are your manners? While Emmy took the honest suggestion and put it to good use."

"Gosh," Phil ruminated, undented by the rebuke, "it was the funniest thing I ever saw."

Emmy's lips twisted toward a smile. "It used to scare Pa."

"You only scared me once, Em." Phil was serious now, and Emmy flushed, understanding what he meant. "Not any more. Everything's going to be okay. Isn't it, Em?"

16

A Journey Short and Long

THE EARLY October darkness had fallen when Phil left Emmy at the door of the Lane tent, and stars were pricking through the soft blue-black sky. Pa had come from work, and Chad had evidently been telling the afternoon's story.

Pa said, "What's all this, missy? Got everything settled, I reckon, you and that young pipsqueak."

Emmy was too warm and happy to bother about the pipsqueak. "Oh, Pa. Oh, Ma. Would you? You would, wouldn't you? Pa, it would do Ma good to stay out the year. She's better already, and think what she'd be if she had a year of it. Much as she'd miss you and Chad."

"Yeh, fine." Pa's tone was heavy with scorn. "Fine for yore ma's health to live in a tent all over snow and down to zero. Okay for you, young and husky and in a nice warm school or rabbit mill all day, to boot. Yeh, fine business."

"But we've got that all figured out," Emmy cried

triumphantly, before the last word had left his lips. "The hermit's shack: you know, Pa. Nobody has any right to it, and we'll move it onto this clearing."

Ma flushed from throat to hairline, but Pa glowered.

"No, sir. No, sir. You can count that out, missy. Lanes never did take other folks' leavings."

She said meekly, "If you can figure out a place for us to live, Pa?"

"Ever strike you that Ma might have some say about it? No say about her only daughter, oh, no. Yo're of age and awful high and mighty all of a sudden. But about herself, and whether she wants to be stuck up here in the snow and ice all winter."

Ma's eyes fell before their triple gaze.

"How about it, Ma?"

"Pa — just one winter — if you and Chad could make out — "

"How about yore ownself? Can you make out without me and Chad?"

Ma's flush deepened. "If — if you come back soon as it's spring, Charlie — "

From that hour plans moved fast, Miss Marthann helping them along. On Saturday morning she was told about the situation. On Saturday noon she sloshed up to the tent, all smiles and galoshes.

"I — believe we've got it. That is, if Mr. Lane approves," she said, her delighted nods taking them all into the conspiracy. "You know those nice new tourist cabins? Little kitchens in a couple of them, and heat and everything?"

Ma and Emmy nodded, spellbound. Chad listened glumly, and so did Pa.

"Well, Mrs. Foster thinks it might pay her to keep them open all winter. Anyway, she wants to give it a try. There's some call for long-term rentals, with the housing shortage, and stranded motorists often stop for the night, this divide catching the winter storms the way it does. Now!" She paused to beam at them — "She and Mr. Foster want to go off to Florida for a winter. Mr. Lane, if you'd be willing to have Mrs. Lane and Emmy move into one of those kitchenette apartments and keep an eye on the rest, the Fosters would be tickled pink."

Pa asked gruffly, "Ain't the rent sky-high?"

"Well, now, this is it: if Emmy wouldn't mind helping Liz clean out after the transients, and if Mrs. Lane and Emmy would keep the keys, then they could have their cabin rent-free till summer."

"Cheap help," Pa grumbled, sliding a glance at Ma.

"You wouldn't think it was too hard, Emmy?" Miss Marthann asked anxiously.

Emmy flexed a muscular young arm. "Hard? For me? Why, I'm right in training, Miss Marthann — Oh, Pa, you'll let us?"

"You don't know when you're being had, missy. No

offense, Miss Marthann. But Ma wouldn't care for such as that, would you, Ma?"

With a nervous hand Ma pushed back the hair from her flushed face. Pretty little Sue Bingham, Emmy thought, her heart tightening. Excitement made Ma's eyes bluer and brighter.

"I'd be there late afternoons and evenings, when folks would stop to inquire," Emmy reassured her —

"For — just one winter, Pa — "

So arrangements rushed on. Pa and Chad and Emmy moved the things Ma wanted into the motel cabin, splashing through slush in the shaded places that were slow to dry. Phil came up with a suggestion. Why couldn't the Lanes start out Monday morning, as usual, he, Phil, following in the coupé? He and Emmy could cut school for one day. That way they could set Pa and Chad on their journey, going as far as Fort Lupton, maybe, and then Phil could bring Ma and Emmy back to the Glen.

After a rather grim silence, Pa said, "Right thoughty of you, young man. Well, if it suits Ma it suits me."

They were all five crowded into the kitchenette apartment as they discussed the plan. Pa ran an appreciative hand over the glowing pine woodwork. "This ain't a bad job of work. But I can't get my breath in no such place. Feel like I was caught in a trap."

Emmy looked around her. "Don't you think Mrs. Foster had real good taste, the colors and all?"

Ma said, "The kitchen — Yellow and green like jonquils — I always thought some day — "

Emmy caught her breath at Ma's words and Ma's expression.

"Sure neat," Phil agreed.

Emmy's attention turned toward him, the more happily because of this new, warm hope Ma's eagerness had im-

planted in her. The boy and girl stood in a doorway and revolved to look into that jonquil kitchen with its small electric range and refrigerator and its lustrous dinette table shoved against the wall, and into the bathroom, shining with chrome and tile.

For Emmy Phil's being here was like a dream. Her brightest imaginings had never quite pictured Phil leaning against the doorway of her house and looking at her like this.

Then Monday was upon them and the little caravan was setting out in the early morning. The day was beautiful, losing its first chill as the sun climbed, and filled with the scent of fallen leaves. Scrub oaks were kindled to russet red by the light, and willows and cottonwoods and narrow-leaf aspen were turning to gold, while sumachs ran down the slopes like red wine.

Here they were, Pa and Ma and Emmy and Chad, swaying, creaking, jouncing along the farmers' road, as they had done so many times before. Sometimes Emmy kept her eyes straight ahead and pretended that she was really going on and on, picking up schools wherever she could, and folding herself over schoolbooks in the back of the truck, crouching under the lantern with them at night. The prospect seemed so real that she had to look back for reassurance.

The green coupé followed close. Everything was all right.

When the two vehicles had traversed the forty-eight miles to Denver and skirted the city to the Fort Lupton road, Phil drew abreast of the truck. "Emmy might ride the rest of the way with me," he suggested, "and let Chad have the seat with his mother."

Silently, Pa put on the brakes and let Emmy swing from truck to coupé. "Bighearted of you, young fellow," he said dryly, his deep-set brown eyes glinting under their black brows.

For a mile or two the young people rode in silence.

"Notice how Pa's driving?" Emmy blurted out at length, shy but laughing, "with one hand?"

"How come?" Phil inquired blankly.

"No wonder you ask. I never saw the like, never. They — they're holding hands."

Phil responded unexpectedly. "I'm left-handed, Em, and that makes it more practical. Try it." Frowning ahead with mock severity, he dropped his hand over hers, on the seat between them. "Gosh," he said huskily, still not looking at her. "Now I see why they do it. It never felt this way to me before."

Emmy blinked down at Phil's hand, big and strong, with nails well shaped, and large enough to look practical, like her own. Somehow it was nice to have their fingernails match.

Phil said, "Your hand feels as beautiful as it looks."

"Beautiful! All scars and callouses?"

"It isn't a baby hand, if that's what you mean."

Emmy slid a quick glance at him. "With the palm like — like crumpled silk? Or like poppy petals just after they've come unpacked from the bud?"

"Just — just exactly," Phil admitted, laughing and blushing.

For a little while they were silent again, Emmy thinking of Abbie and Abbie's baby hands; thinking that it was like being in a home of her own, to have her hand in Phil's, quiet and warm.

"But, Phil," she said hesitantly, "hadn't we better let this be — all?"

"Once in a while a good-night kiss?" Phil protested. "Everybody does, Emmy."

"I don't give a hoot what everyone does." Emmy was breathing hard, partly because she was thinking that Abbie was "everybody." "Seems like kisses — seems like they oughtn't to get common — like they ought to be kept for a person's home. If home's like I've imagined, everything ought to be — be saved up for it."

"You almost worship the idea of a home, Em."

"And besides that, if you edge in too close to danger — "

Phil nodded soberly. "I know. It can easy get too strong for you — reach out and grab you. Only most girls look at it a lot different."

He began again. "Once in a long while? A kiss, I mean. Now that we're going steady." The coupé lurched — "I'm not haywire, Emmy? We are going steady, aren't we?"

Emmy couldn't answer, because her breath had suddenly left her.

"Em! That Spanish Cavalier of yours — ?"

His anxiety was so exhilarating that Emmy was tempted to tease him a little. But she couldn't. As soon as she could speak, she said, "I'll write and tell Andrés. Though our not coming has told him already. And I wasn't ever promised to Andrés. Or to anybody else." She gulped another mouthful of breath before she could add: "Not till this minute, Phil."

Phil still did not look at her, but the coupé gave an indignant jump, and Phil's hand tightened on hers till it hurt, a good hurt. "Emmy," he asked abruptly, "you do like cattle, don't you?"

Though Emmy thought concern underlay his mock-anxious tone, she chose to respond to the surface humor. She needed to have the talk lightened, for she had never felt like this before, floating in happiness, yet anchored in something as solid as granite.

"Why, Phil," she said, "I never really met any. Not socially. You might say I'd just had a passing acquaintance, like when a bull chased me out of a field where I was picking flowers, but I'm sure I could dote on them if I had a good chance."

Silent again, they rode on. Emmy thought if she were to open her mouth again she might shout or sing or say something silly.

For here she was, Emmy Lane, the basket girl, smooth and clean and getting educated, and settled for the winter in a smooth clean little house. Here she was, Emmy Lane, on her way to college and to a ranch house. Even more amazing, here she was with a whole shining world of wonder and possibility before her and Phil. Phil.

That future shone still more dazzling by contrast when truck and coupé rattled across the tracks and pulled up in the farm labor camp at Fort Lupton. The first person they saw was Mrs. Lucero, solidly round and waddling a little as she carried water to tin cans of geraniums which she had set outside for a sunning.

It was noon, and it seemed the Luceros were topping beets near at hand, for they began to appear almost at once, trooping home for dinner. The big ones joined the little ones in swarming over the truck, while Refugio scurried joyfully to Emmy, who jumped out of the coupé with Phil following her.

"You and him that way?" Refugio murmured eagerly, when Emmy had made the introductions. "But you don't need to tell me, Emmy. It shines out all over you."

Emmy smiled rather absently at Refugio, her eyes darting from one to another of the swarm of Luceros. "Andrés — ?" she asked —

"He stay behind in California."

"Eufemia Martinez?"

"*Verdad.*" Refugio slipped into Spanish for her affirmative. "You never came, Emmy. So he know — but here comes somebody," she broke off with relief. "Paco! Please come meet my girl friend. Emmy, here is my husband," she added, picking a bit of grass from his shoulder with proprietary pride.

"You two going to settle down somewhere?" Emmy asked hopefully, when she had mastered her surprise. "You will have a home, won't you, Refugio?"

Refugio shrugged daintily. "What for? Both of us working in the crops; we don' make bad money, Emmy. And seems like it would be awful dull — "

At last the goodbyes were all said, and Emmy and Ma and Phil were on their way back to the Glen. Emmy's silence had changed, as if some of the glow and glory had oozed out of it. At length Phil frowned sidewise at her, and looked beyond her at Ma. Ma sat in her characteristic loose huddle, lost to all that passed around her. Yet Ma's look had changed, too. Her cheeks glistened as with tears, and her eyes had lost some of their dull blankness.

"Emmy." Phil spoke hoarsely.

"What, Phil?"

"Emmy, look at me. This minute. Are you — feeling bad — about that Spanish Cavalier?"

Vigorously Emmy shook her head, eyes widening in surprise. "That news about Andrés was the best I could have had. It's Refugio. And the others."

"Refugio? Why, Refugio looks as happy as a kitten."

Emmy spoke with repressed intensity. "Phil, she doesn't have the least idea what there is to life. It's all closed to her, the way it was years ago to me. And it's not much better for her younger brothers and sisters. Oh, the Center, and Girl Scouts and Boy Scouts, might give Margarita and some of the rest a lift, because they haven't settled into quite so much of a pattern. But it's harder than ever for them to get schooling. And there aren't enough Centers, like the ones at Conchita and Fort Lupton; not enough workers. Looks as if most of the kids are going on like their fathers and mothers before them."

"But, Em, you can't help it if they haven't the get-up and go to — to demand an education and all the rest of it."

"Can't I, Phil?" Emmy asked soberly. "Maybe I could if I'd set my mind to it. Instead of that, I'm thinking of nothing but — but us, and college and our — our ranch house." Reddening and feeling dizzy at the admission, she hurried on. "Oughtn't I to work for them, like Miss Kay and Miss Amy and those college kids that help them? I might be able to get hold in a different way — because I've been in their shoes. I know that they're just folks, like the rest of us." Emmy turned appealingly to Phil.

Phil's mouth was a firm, straight line, his chin jutting squarely below it, and his gray eyes narrowed with concentration on this new outlook.

All of a sudden, Phil's grown up, Emmy thought. Under his kid ways — why, he's a man.

"Honey," he asked gently, "can't we tell better after we've gone through Aggies? What we ought to do?"

"But would I have the grit? You took notice how I've — I've already moved into — into our ranch house. Phil, I already put up apricot curtains, like Miss Marty's."

"Gosh, Emmy. Gosh. To hear you say that! But listen, hon. You just said yourself that college kids helped Miss Kay. In the summer, and without pay, I take it. We might figure out a way to work half time at a regular job and the other half at one of the Centers. Maybe a few good summers would be doing our bit, Em?"

Our bit. We. In our broadening, deepening, heightening world. In our shining world.

"Phil," she said huskily, "you know something? You're wonderful."